A Little Night Fishing

By Chuck Daukas

Damnation Books, LLC.
P.O. Box 3931
Santa Rosa, CA 95402-9998
www.damnationbooks.com

A Little Night Fishing
by Chuck Daukas
Second Edition

Digital ISBN: 978-1-62929-117-8
Print ISBN: 978-1-62929-118-5

Cover art by: Dawné Dominique
Edited by: Trevor Donaldson

Copyright 2014 Chuck Daukas

Printed in the United States of America
Worldwide Electronic & Digital Rights
Worldwide English Language Print Rights

All rights reserved. No part of this book may be reproduced, scanned or distributed in any form, including digital and electronic or mechanical, including photocopying, recording, or by any information storage and retrieval system, without the prior written consent of the Publisher, except for brief quotes for use in reviews.

This book is a work of fiction. Characters, names, places and incidents either are the product of the author's imagination or are used fictitiously, and any resemblance to any actual persons, living or dead, events, or locales is entirely coincidental.

*Dedicated to:
My pals on the South Shore of RI—
group hug for all.*

*I wish to thank my editor and
writing mentor, Paul Eno for his
insights, thoughtfulness, generosity,
and experience that lifted A Little
Night Fishing to an entirely new
level. Thanks also to Martha
Nichols for her editing and insights.*

Chapter One

Ralph Hunley suppressed a strong urge to shout curses into the soggy twilight as he stood on the fog-shrouded jetty. On an evening as still as this one, a screaming voice surely would have attracted attention, but attention was the last thing Hunley wanted. Instead, he quietly pulled out a knife, and with grim determination silently plunged it into the source of his anger.

Problem solved.

He then pulled the wild snarl of fishing line from his pole and dropped it carelessly to the side. This was his first cast of the evening—a cast abruptly halted in mid-flight by the massive tangle that suddenly burst from his reel.

Mishap number one, Hunley thought.

His second cast reminded him how important it was to clean a fishing reel after it sat all winter. He failed to notice that the bridge didn't click into place when cocked back, and during the cast, it slipped into its locked position. With the ugly, but oh-so-familiar snap of a line breaking under too much strain, Hunley found himself watching his brand new lure soar into the fog like a flying fish.

Mishap number two.

Amazing how much farther a plug can go without a line attached to it, he thought after hearing the doleful splash in the mist.

"Nine bucks down the drain, but it doesn't bother me. Nothing's going to get in the way of a nice evening of fishing," Hunley said to the fog.

It had been a rotten day. His girlfriend told him to take a hike. He got his report card in the mail, saying he didn't pass algebra and either had to go to summer school or not graduate. Then, he collided head-first into a parked car while trying to impress a group of kids with his skateboarding skills. Not only did Hunley leave an impression on them, he left one on the car, too. So, he'd looked forward to spending this Friday evening out on his favorite fishing spot—the west jetty of

Tuckernut Breachway, on the south shore of Rhode Island.

Summer vacation was less than a week old, and he would enjoy this private time before the bustle of trips to the beach, movies, illegal drinking parties, and maybe even finding a new girl, summer school or no summer school.

Just relax and enjoy right now. The summer's just beginning.

Slicing fifty yards into the Atlantic Ocean, the eastern and western jetties formed the boundaries of a channel that connected a large salt pond to the ocean. The jetty bordered Tuckernut Beach, whose waves broke well before the shore as they rolled in, making for great body surfing when the waves were big enough. The jetty's channel sported swift currents that stirred up the food supply for the stripers and bluefish. There was always good fishing from these rocks, even though it was still very early in the season.

Though, the jetty was different this year. Hurricane Sandy blasted its way through here last fall, actually lifting two of the massive, fitted blocks of granite out from where they nestled undisturbed since the jetty was built sixty years ago and many hurricanes later, dumping them atop the neighboring rocks. The other rocks all slightly shifted and no longer provided a flat surface to stand or walk on. When wet, it was much easier to slip than it used to be. The jetty literally felt different. It was a little easier to get hurt out here.

Hunley stared at the massive, displaced boulders and tried to imagine the power of the waves that accomplished such a feat. Right where he was standing. A chill of uneasiness swept through his body.

Feelin' kinda' small and insignificant.

"Okay," he said quietly to himself to stop his imagination from going any further. "Fishing. Unwind and relax." He filled his lungs with the wet, ocean air and smiled.

Ralph Hunley also believed that tonight, he would catch his first keeper of the year. Luck or no luck, just being out fishing was enough for him. Best of all, he had the entire jetty to himself, while on the eastern jetty, three fishermen competed for space. The only sounds of the evening were a muffled voice now and then from one of those fishermen, the gentle sloshing of an occasional swell against the rocks, and the intermittent moan of the distant Watch Hill foghorn. He finally began to unwind. Even a tangled line was less frustrating than having some blabbermouth fishing next to you. To him, fishing was quiet hour, not social hour. Banal conversation with strangers had the same effect on his nerves as an incessantly barking dog.

Hunley opened his tackle box. In spite of the increasing darkness, there was still enough light to see into the jumble of lures and fishing plugs. Spotting the blue and white popper, "Old Faithful" as he called it, he reached into the box, felt a sharp jab, and cursed out loud for not keeping his tackle better organized. A drop of blood welled up from the prick in his finger.

With his lucky popper finally clipped onto the very light-gauge line, Hunley cast into the swirling fog. Although he couldn't make out the plug's splash in the fog and fading light, he could easily hear its ker-plunk.

"Ker-plunk," he murmured.

The sea was almost flat calm, as though the blanket of fog was too heavy for waves to rise beneath its weight. Yet, the tide surged into the Breachway, the current in the channel already more powerful than when Hunley had first arrived. Stationary waves quickly built at the Breachway's mouth, their crests turning into gurgling whitecaps as they collapsed upon themselves.

For a moment, Hunley fancied the whitecaps as the teeth of a giant shark, and the water racing into the Breachway reminded him of a scene in a television documentary, where a huge great white was cruising on the surface with its mouth wide open. What had struck Hunley was the huge volume of seawater rushing over its jagged teeth and pouring into its cavernous maw, to then stream out its massive gills at the rate of at least one barrel per second.

What an ugly creature...and what a way to die!

The chill in the air became penetrating, and Hunley found himself wishing that he'd brought a heavier jacket. The fog swirled thicker still. The silhouettes of the three fishermen on the other jetty blended more and more with the texture of the evening, making them seem like apparitions slowly fading out of Hunley's dimension of time and space. Land was no longer visible. The jetty disappeared into the inky murk, making it easy for him to imagine being on a rock in the middle of the ocean.

"Not feeling attached to the land," he whispered.

Hunley remembered a recurring nightmare, finding himself in the middle of the sea at night in a tiny, rubber raft. He would think of the thousands of feet of black ocean beneath him, and that the only thing keeping the water from sucking him down was the thin, air-filled rubber membrane. That's when the wind would pick up and the waves start to build...

A sudden movement startled him. Shadows scurried among the rocks! Rats? A chill of revulsion shot up Hunley's spine. As his eyes picked out the shadows, he quickly realized that they weren't moving, and when he looked closely, he saw all that they were—shadows among the rocks. Hunley realized that his imagination was getting out of hand, something that happened to him more than he would like to admit when fishing alone at night.

"Okay!" he chirped to the fog, trying to bring his thoughts under control. The sound of his own voice startled him as it cut into the socked-in stillness. He shook his head and smiled. "Think fishing, Ralph," he said, daring the silence. "Casting into an oncoming current is a recipe for tangled lines unless I reel it in quickly," he continued, pretending that he was the expert commentator in one of the fishing shows he occasionally watched.

"In conditions like this, it's always best to use a heavy swimming lure with a swift uptake of your line. But I always have the best luck when I use a surface plug and light tackle—very light tackle. The plug I'm using now isn't an ordinary surface plug. It's my lucky surface plug. I always catch something with it! I'll risk another tangle or snapped line if it also increases my chance to catch a big fish!"

Ralph Hunley really did have a strong feeling that tonight he was going to strike it big.

The lingering twilight finally gave itself up to the darkness, and his private island seemed even smaller. The only illumination was on shore, where the miasma made the distant lights of the parking lot glow a pale orange. The foghorn sang. From the glow, a silhouette suddenly appeared. Another fisherman.

"Hell," Hunley muttered.

As the angler approached, Hunley noted that he was very tall and built like a football player. In spite of the raw air, he was wearing only a T-shirt and shorts, with nothing on his feet.

A Little Night Fishing

Oh great. A weirdo, no less.

The guy carried a pole and a bucket, and he had a long-handled gaff strapped to his belt. His gait was sure-footed over the moist rocks. He walked without a sound.

"Howdy!" the man greeted jovially, but in a weird, loud, guttural voice that made Hunley's muscles tense.

"Hello," Hunley responded, trying not to sound nervous.

"Beautiful night! Absolutely beautiful! Yep. Nothin' beats fishin' in the fog!"

Hunley made himself smile politely.

"Oops, doesn't look like you've been havin' much luck there, bud!" the intruder rumbled as he noticed the tangle of fishing line at the boy's feet.

Again, Hunley tried to smile, but it was more of a grimace. "Maybe you'll bring me good luck," he forced himself to say.

That was when Hunley realized that the huge man was dripping wet, as though he'd just come out of the water.

"Oh, yeah!" The man laughed. "You might be right! Y'know, I got a way with catchin' fish!"

Hunley cast his lucky popper. It hit the water with another forlorn ker-plunk.

When Hunley began reeling in his line, the man boomed, "Y'know, bud. Your line's prob'ly gonna get tangled if you don't reel your plug in faster."

"Uh huh," Hunley responded, feeling again that primal twinge of warning.

"I'm serious, pal. That current comin' your way's gonna make your uptake too loose in your reel."

Hunley reeled his line in faster. He looked across the channel to the eastern jetty, now barely a shadow, and he found himself wishing he'd chosen that side to fish on. That was when he realized it was vacant. He peered hard into the mist and found that all three fishermen were gone. It was as though they'd fled like fish into the gloom on sensing a predator.

The enormous man pulled a twelve-inch menhaden, or "bunker", from his bucket and cut it into thirds, baited his hook with the speed and skill of a veteran, and cast far into the darkness. The man's pole immediately bent violently. A strike!

"Oh, yeah!" he chortled. "Got him!"

Hunley couldn't believe it.

"He's a big one, all right. Bluefish! Ha! Ha!"

In no time, the intruder expertly landed the biggest bluefish Hunley had ever seen. Its tiny, dagger-like teeth chomped down on the hook that protruded from its bleeding mouth as it thrashed on the rocks.

"Well, well. These guys have pretty sharp teeth, now don't they?" he asked with a taunting edge to his rumbling voice. "But these teeth are nothin' compared to real fish!"

Real fish? thought Hunley. *What the hell is that supposed to mean?*

He kept cranking in his line while keeping one eye on the intruder and his catch.

"Bluefish like to think they're tough guys," the man continued as he watched the fish flap and flail desperately at his feet. "You don't seem so tough to me now, fishy." With his fingers hooked into the fish's gills, he raised its face to an inch from his own.

"Now talk, shithead! Were you alone or in a school? *Answer me!* You were in a school, weren't you? *Weren't you!* How many in your school? What direction they headed?"

He shook the fish. "Won't talk, will you?"

Under other circumstances, Hunley would have thought the intruder's little skit hilarious. Now, he only wished he'd picked a different place to fish.

"Ve haff vays of making you talk," the giant mocked. He gently laid the flapping fish on the wet rocks. "Now, tell me: How many in your school?"

Like lightning, the fisherman slammed his gaff down on the fish. It hit with a thud, and the fish bucked in agony.

"How many?" he suddenly screamed. "Where's the school, now? Where are they goin'? How deep are they?" He grabbed the hook, still in the fish's mouth, and began twisting it. "Talk! Sign zee papers, old man!"

The fish thrashed.

Then, Hunley watched the man stick his huge fingers inside the bluefish's mouth, as if to pull out the hook. Hunley opened his mouth to warn him of the bluefish's razor-like teeth. "Uhh..." But his warning stuck in his throat.

Predictably, the fish's jaws snapped into the man's finger. He made no sound of pain, and casually extracted his bleeding finger from the fish's teeth, ripping the wound open even more. He gently laid the fish on the rocks.

"Bluefish," the man spat with quiet hatred as he raised the

A Little Night Fishing

gaff high above his head, "have a fuckin' attitude problem!"

He swung the gaff down with blinding speed and smashed it into the fish's head with rage that was terrifying. There was a hollow *crunch*! The fish's skull instantly imploded under the impact, the sound slicing into the foggy night.

Stunned, Hunley winced as he watched the man again raise the gaff high over his head, then swing it down savagely...again and again. With enraged abandon, the maniac screamed, "I'll fuckin' kill you! I'll fuckin' kill you!" as scales and fish blood splattered into the air and pooled on the rocks.

"Oh...my...God!" blurted Hunley, staring in frozen fascination.

Breathing heavily, the intruder knelt next to the fish and grabbed the hook still caught in what was left of its mouth. He yanked it out, taking the fish's entire lower jaw with it. He looked up at Hunley, noticed his look of shock, and smiled. Silhouetted against the dull glow behind him, the only feature that Hunley could make out in the darkness was the man's teeth.

Hunley's heart pounded, and his mouth became dry.

I'll just take one more cast, then casually pick up my stuff, walk around this lunatic, and get the hell out of here. It's definitely time to leave!

As Hunley readied his rod for the final cast, he saw out of the corner of his eye that the madman was cutting another piece of bait and putting it on his hook. The next thing Hunley noticed was the man raising his fingers to his mouth. Hunley couldn't tell for certain, but he got the impression that the guy licked them.

I hope I don't catch anything, he thought as he absently cocked the bridge of the reel back and pinched the line with a trembling index finger.

He raised the pole over his shoulder, then jerked it forward. Instantly, the bridge slipped, locking the line in mid-cast. The line snapped with an ugly sound, and his lucky popper went soaring off into the night. A lonely ker-plunk was the last sound it ever made as the ocean swallowed it whole.

"I told you!" There was no trace of humor in the man's rumble. "Did you listen to me? No, because you somehow have this fuckin' idea that you know more about fishin' than I do. It seems to me, girlie-boy, that *you've* got an attitude problem, too!"

The image of his lucky popper sinking to the cold ocean floor swam before Hunley, and the strategic reality that this lunatic was much bigger than he was, and stood between him and land, sank very much into his mind. The man cast his line out.

"Yeah!" he whooped as his pole lurched over violently.

Oh, Jesus...

"Yep! This one's a striper...and a big one!" He jerked the pole back hard to set the hook, then held it in one hand. He leered at Hunley and boomed, "Hey, look Mom! One hand!"

Hunley stood there blank-faced, purposely avoiding the man's gaze. The lunatic glared at him with stiletto-like eyes while his pole shook with the struggling fish. Time stopped. The foghorn howled.

"Boy, I sure love to eat striped bass," the angler from hell suddenly roared as time resumed, and he began cranking in his line. "But they're definitely cowards when it comes to fightin'."

Cowards? Hunley thought blankly as he looked at the wild tangle of fishing line at his feet.

He realized that his hands were shaking, and something urged him to just drop the pole and run. Before he could flee, the maniac easily landed the fish—a thirty-pound striped bass, dripping wet and flapping on the rocks. The man picked up the gaff, and Hunley groaned. The fisherman smiled, set the gaff down, and gently worked the hook out of the striper's mouth.

"He looks so good, I think I'll eat him right here!" he burbled.

The man tilted his head back as he lifted the struggling fish over his mouth. His jaws opened. His eyes rolled backward, and white inner eyelids slid over them.

Hunley froze in horror as he watched the fisherman's mouth open as wide as humanly possible, only to continue to open wider and wider, until both jaws literally disconnected from their joints. His maw gaped wider and wider, his eyes blank white, and Hunley knew that he was in a waking nightmare.

"No..." Hunley choked as the thing's sharp, inhumanly triangular teeth glistened and its jaws yawned still wider, its face a grisly distortion.

"I'm not seeing this..." Hunley groaned in utter shock as

the head of the struggling fish disappeared into the giant's now cavernous mouth. The creature's neck, then its entire body, began lurching in spasms as it worked the massive fish into its gullet.

"Oh, God!" Hunley moaned as the intruder's entire body heaved violently. The thirty-pound fish squeezed down and down into its stomach until only the tail was sticking out of its chops. Then, the monster's eyes cleared and looked Hunley straight in the eye. It bit off the fish's tail with a loud *chomp!*

With one last heave of the creature's gullet, the fish disappeared inside its now swollen bulk.

"All gone!" it gurgled, spreading its arms while holding the fish's tail in its hand, its voice wet and distorted as the jaws slid back into their joints. "Though, I can't stand this part!" It tossed the tail at Hunley's feet.

Oh God! Oh God! Oh God!

The boy's mind raced insanely, and every instinct in him screamed.

Your life is in danger! Your life is in danger! Danger!

Standing between Hunley and land, with its engorged midsection heaving and bulging as the huge fish continued to squirm inside its stomach, the monster watched Hunley like a cat eying a bird with a broken wing.

Gotta deal with it! Oh, God...deal with it!

"I know what you're thinking!" the creature ululated. "You're thinking, 'Wow! How did he do that? Boy, he sure is talented!'"

Hunley's lips quivered. Tears streamed down his face.

"Aw, you're upset," mocked the intruder. "Is it because I didn't eat the tail?"

It waited for an answer, staring Hunley down.

"You think that I'm bein' wasteful. Is that it? You're thinkin' of all those poor children in the world who won't ever get the chance to eat a fishie's tail, aren't you?" the monster uttered in a sickening, inhuman purr.

"Well, since you feel that way, asshole. You eat it!" it suddenly roared.

Just as suddenly, the knife lurched into Hunley's tormented mind.

He spotted it lying on the rocks between him and the monster. The monster saw it, too. Hunley lunged for it, but he slipped on the slick blood and slime of the slaughtered bluefish, crying out as he landed face down on the rocks, breaking two of his upper front teeth. Right before Hunley's eyes, the monster casually stepped on the knife with a bare foot and glared down at Hunley with amusement.

"Oh, my goodness. Did you hurt yourself?" it asked with bogus concern.

Pain shot through Hunley's jaw as he tasted his own blood and spat out pieces of his teeth. He pushed himself up from the gore-splattered rocks. He began to sob.

"Aw, there—there, now. Come 'ere, and let me give you a nice hug," the creature soothed, then boomed: "Group hug, everybody! Come and get it!"

Hunley darted to the left side of the jetty, but the thing jumped playfully to that side to block his route.

"Oops! That way won't work!" The creature guffawed. Hunley started for the other side, but the behemoth hopped in his way again, like a puppy about to intercept a rolling ball.

"Nope. Not that way, either," it bubbled gleefully.

Hunley glanced at the black water. The current washed strongly shoreward, the whitecaps of the stationary waves sloshing loudly.

"Don't even think about that!" the monster warned.

Without hesitation, Hunley plunged into the swift water. The shock of the cold punched the air out of his lungs as the sea swallowed him. He quickly thrashed to the surface, gasping for air as the current carried him swiftly into the Breachway. His sneakers sliced heavily through the water, like rocks pulling him down.

"Help!" Hunley screamed. "Hel—" The swirling current sucked him under.

"I'll save you!" the monster chortled as Hunley again burst to the surface, gagging. He heard a large, sickening splash behind him.

It's in the water! Oh, God...it's in the water! Oh, God... should'a taken my sneakers off... Oh, God...it's cold! Oh, God!

He flailed as the current whisked him down the Breachway, far enough down for him to make out streetlights and the parking lot through the fog. Salvation was in sight! He stroked harder and faster. Just then, his hand brushed against a large, rough object that suddenly cut in front of him. Then, an enormous dorsal fin sliced through the water just a few feet before his stunned eyes.

A Little Night Fishing

Oh, God! Just head to the rocks! Oh, God! Head to the rocks! You're going to make it...oh, God!

Suddenly, the creature's head—half shark, half human—popped out of the water right in front of him.

"*Boo!*" it roared, then disappeared back into the blackness.

Ahead, concrete steps reached down to the water.

Ten feet!

Five feet!

One foot!

Hunley shrieked as two rows of knives bit through his flesh, seizing his ankles like a bear trap, snapping both Achilles' tendons. The shark gently tugged him away from the rocks, and Hunley frantically thrashed his arms in front of him, desperately trying to keep his face out of the water. The shark let go, and Hunley sucked air into his lungs as he again splashed toward the steps.

Ten feet!

Five feet!

One foot! Got it!

Just as his frigid hands clutched the slippery step, Hunley shrieked as the trap-like jaws slammed shut around his ankles, again. He gasped for air but sucked in seawater. He coughed, vomited, and swallowed more water. Spasms wracked his body. A prickly, carbonated darkness quickly seeped into Hunley's mind. He felt himself start to separate from his body, and he suddenly became calm.

Ralph Hunley's final, cogent thought was the realization that his head had passed between rows of teeth and that he was inside the shark. He could feel the slimy flesh surround him and then begin squeezing him further in until his head pressed into the shark's gullet, which opened and began to suck him down. As he passed, violent contractions worked him further inside its body, and he realized in a matter-of-fact way that he had been swallowed whole. He wondered whether sharks had bad breath, and then found it funny that he would think such a thing at a time like this.

The last physical sensation his body ever registered was a tremendous jolt of pain, and Ralph Hunley's last thought as a human being was the realization that his feet had just been bitten off.

Chapter Two

Just arrived from North Carolina, an elderly couple walked their white toy poodle along a quiet Tuckernut road by the shoreline. It was a beautiful morning. They stopped to enjoy the panorama of beach and rocky coast stretching below them. Suddenly, their attention snapped to a commotion in the water about fifty yards offshore. A skin diver was struggling desperately on the surface. Even from this distance, they could catch an unearthly sound. It was the diver screaming in agony through his snorkel.

"Oh, m'God! We gotta call for help!" the woman cried.

Both realized with horror that they had left their cell phones back at the cottage, and the nearest house was two hundred yards away.

Throbbing with pain, Bob Brickley tried to shake his finger from the iron grip of the enraged blue crab, whose claw bit effortlessly through his gloved hand and sliced into his flesh. The creature stubbornly refused to let go. Only when Brickley thrust his hand out of the water and slammed it repeatedly against the surface did the crab finally bail. A tiny cloud of blood seeped from the wound into the ocean. With his heart pounding violently and adrenaline surging through his veins, Brickley blew out the seawater that had flooded his snorkel during the struggle, glanced at the blood seeping from the gash in his glove, and pretended that he wasn't worried about sharks picking up the scent.

Still clutched firmly in Brickley's unwounded hand was his brand new spear gun, out for its trial mission. He'd finagled some extra hours at his summer job to get the money to buy it. For the past three days, he'd spent much time simply admiring it, daydreaming about the trophies it would bring him, and about his first time out with it.

What will my first fish be? A tautaug? Striper? Flounder?

For over a year, Brickley drooled over the spear gun's picture in an online catalog. Now, he held it in his hands. It was top-of-the-line, and he hoped its first victim would be a big striped bass, although he'd certainly settle for a tasty blackfish if one turned up. Considering the poor visibility in these waters, his intended victim would appear so suddenly that he would have only a second to judge whether it was above the size limit, then to aim and fire.

In his hurry to get to the water, Brickley had forgotten his diver's flag and buoy, which should have been attached by a line to his spear gun.

Stupid! he thought.

He had to be at work in less than two hours, so rather than go back, he decided to risk it.

The current was stronger than Tuckernut's summer "rent-a-cop" expected. The water was murkier, too, in spite of the calm sea. The current whisked him steadily over and around weed-shrouded rocks, barely distinguishable shadows until he was about to collide with them. Suddenly, a rogue whitecap surged over him, slapping him against a rock he hadn't realized was there. Brickley sucked water into his snorkel, and adrenaline surged through his body again as he pushed himself away, his hand still smarting from that crazy crab.

Another whitecap broke, spinning Brickley sideways, where he came face-to-face with the outstretched claws of yet another blue crab perched on the side of yet another rock. He desperately pushed himself off, flipped over on his back, and kicked his fins violently. The rock, with its scrappy crab, quickly disappeared into the murk. Chills ran up Brickley's spine as a stream of intensely cold seawater trickled down the neck of his wet-suit and ran down his back.

Brickley wondered how badly he was bleeding. Was he leaving a trail of blood? He remembered that there was only one documented shark attack in Rhode Island waters in the previous 340 years. Still, there were sand sharks, tiger sharks, sandbar sharks, dogfish, and the occasional great white around here, with blue sharks, makos, and threshers farther out...and who knew what else?

A hundred yards down current, a pair of giant nostrils sampled the seawater and tasted Bob Brickley's blood.

The current carried Brickley steadily toward the outermost extension of the rock reef, known simply as "The Point". Here, the current collided with still water, and it was the roughest part of the journey—the part Brickley hated most. It was the part where he would bite hard on his snorkel's mouthpiece and kick as hard as he could to get through. This place always shook him up. It was always here that he would be confronted with the fact that the ocean had a way of scaring the hell out of him at certain moments. To soothe his ego, Brickley called it "respect".

Around The Point and the reef, he had about a ten-minute swim to cross Tuckernut Beach and arrive at his destination—the outer rocks of Tuckernut Breachway. As it was illegal to dive directly from the rocks of the breachway itself, it could only be accessed by swimming. Time was ticking away, and soon, Bob's favorite spear fishing spot would be closed for swimming only until 6:00 that evening.

With a slow swish of its tail, the twelve-foot shark glided casually toward the source of the blood. Despite the low visibility, the animal could easily sense the swimmer by the vibrations his strokes generated in the water. It knew exactly how big and how stressed he was.

Bob Brickley's heart beat faster as the current picked up speed. The rising surface chop jolted him back and forth, up and down, as nausea started oozing into his stomach.

God, I hate this part, he thought.

Brickley hadn't spent his years playing football at Easterly High School and, more recently, the University of Rhode Island, for nothing. His well-muscled legs kicked powerfully through the swirling water, seaweed, silt, and ominous shadows. Big, brown-haired, and painfully shy, Brickley was a fourth-grade teacher at Tuckernut Elementary School. He didn't have much chance to exercise in that job, so diving had become a summer passion.

Then, Brickley saw it. Like a writhing eel, a rope slithered upward to a barnacle-coated buoy, marking the outermost tip of the rock reef. He kept a sharp ear for the whine of a boat engine, and he regretted the decision not to return home for his diver's flag. It would be easy for one of those damned jet skis to pancake him.

With this spear gun, it would be even easier for me to harpoon one, he thought with wry satisfaction. Sticking his head out of the water several times to get his bearings, Brickley crossed the mouth of Tuckernut Beach far enough off shore to avoid any swimmers and the wrath of the lifeguard, then angled toward the jetty and stopped about twenty-feet from the man-made wall of rocks. He flipped off the spear gun's safety catch, pressed the butt of the weapon against his shoulder, and took aim. He would simply float here and wait for something to swim by.

It didn't take long.

The shadow seemed as large as the rocks he'd been dodging only moments before, but this shadow moved—toward him. Bob Brickley suddenly found himself face-to-face with the largest striped bass he'd ever seen. His heart pounded as he gently aimed. He pulled the trigger. The shaft shrieked through the water and slammed into the fish with a sickening thud, and a cloud of blood and scales burst from the wound.

"Anticlimax" was precisely the way to describe Brickley's feelings on seeing the gory results of his deed. For, despite his weight-lifter build and athletic background, Bob Brickley was a gentle soul, retiring and bookish. The beautiful fish now destroyed. Brickley's grip on the spear gun eased as his guilt tightened, and the next thing he knew, his brand new, match-quality spear gun slipped from his grasp. He shot out a frantic hand, but his fingertips barely touched the weapon before it slid away as the dying fish found one last surge of strength.

Oh, shit!

Brickley kicked like a madman, but the spear gun sank toward the bottom. One more agonized swish from the bass's tail, and both disappeared into the murk. Water churned at the surface as Brickley kicked his finned feet furiously in a desperate attempt to catch up with the spear gun, but it wasn't going to happen. It was a goner. In utter disbelief, Brickley floated motionlessly.

It might have been another minute, during which Brickley contemplated sucking seawater into his lungs and ending it all, when the nervous little ker-plunk of a pebble slapping the water only feet from him broke his suicidal reverie. Another pebble hit the water, this time only a foot from his face. He took a deep breath, let it out slowly through his snorkel, then cried out in shock as a third pebble beaned his wetsuit-hooded head.

Brickley broke the surface and swung toward shore, wanting to take the spear gun he couldn't believe was gone and skewer the moron who was pelting him with rocks. Then, he saw not just a moron, but The Moron. It was a gloating, hulking police sergeant. More specifically, it was Sergeant Alphonse Fergosi.

"Sorry, Mister Rent-A-Cop!" Fergosi taunted. "I didn't mean to hit you!"

Brickley heard the frantic wail of sirens approaching as he clambered onto the rocks of Tuckernut Breachway, yanked off his flippers, and faced the man he detested most in the world.

"How did you know where to find me?" a very annoyed Bob Brickley asked.

"It's my job to know these things, Chief. Now, I bring two items of business," Fergosi announced with a smirk. "First, we just had a report of a diver in distress. That wouldn't be you, would it?"

"No," Brickley answered honestly. "I'm fine."

"Ah," replied Fergosi.

The sirens screamed louder and louder.

"Chief," Fergosi continued with mock gravity, "the Town of Easterly needs your help. We have a problem that only you can solve!"

The sarcasm was as subtle as a fishhook through the foot. As it was, Brickley's ego still throbbed from dropping the spear gun. He silently cursed all creation, and especially Sergeant Shithead, as the sirens became a deafening din. Suddenly pouring into the Tuckernut Beach parking lot was the source of the sirens: an ambulance screeched to a halt, followed by a rescue vehicle, fire truck, and a state Department of Environmental Management Jeep. Doors opened and slammed shut, and leading a pack of uniformed and very serious-looking men was a man well into his senior years.

"There he is!" the old man shouted, pointing at Brickley.

They filed down the jetty rocks and surrounded the embarrassed diver, firing questions at him. Bob assured them that he was okay. It was the environmental police officer's question that he was hoping wouldn't be asked.

"Where's your dive flag?"

As quickly as they arrived, they departed. The now-soaked ticket tucked under Brickley's still-dripping sleeve informed him that he owed the State of Rhode Island and Providence Plantations fifty dollars, along with a court summons.

Fergosi shook his head with amusement.

"Now, where were we? Oh yeah, the possible missing person..."

* * * *

A Little Night Fishing

Yes, Brickley, as the summer security officer for the Village of Tuckernut, made a security patrol in the village last night. Yes, he'd noticed a car of the kind belonging to the missing person. Indeed, it was parked over in Tuckernut Breachway's lot. Fergosi told Brickley that the car was still there, but that there was no sign of its owner—a local high school kid named Ralph Hunley. When he hadn't come home last night, his hysterical mother reported him missing. They found no clothes and no fishing equipment. Maybe the guy was off someplace with friends. Maybe he was dead. Who knew?

Bob Brickley acted annoyed that Fergosi was bothering him with this, but in fact, he was intensely interested. In college, when other kids were out getting smashed, Brickley would be in his dorm room for hours, engrossed in detective stories or TV mysteries. His idol: Sherlock Holmes—something he'd never dare tell Sergeant Moron.

Brickley also loved classical music, which didn't do much for his social life, either.

If there was foul play, last night's rain would have washed away any signs of blood, Brickley thought as he picked his way along the rocks of the west jetty, not yet dubbed a crime scene—so far.

Fergosi watched him with amused disdain. "Maybe, you can be 'Mister Rent-A-Detective'!" he chirped. "Well, I'm outta here. It sure has been fun!"

Brickley ignored The Moron as Fergosi moved his bulk over the rocks, toward the parking lot.

All of a sudden, he nearly tripped over the fly-covered tail of a very large striped bass. His wet-suit still dripping, he knelt to examine it and wondered why no gull or rat had eaten it. Brickley searched the nearby cracks and crevasses for the rest of the carcass but found nothing. Then, he noticed something even more unusual. The tail hadn't been sliced cleanly with a knife. No knife would leave this type of ragged, V-shaped cut. The first thing Brickley thought of was a shark bite. Of course, that was absurd, but no brighter idea came to him.

As he stood there pondering, the sight of his sinking spear gun suddenly swam before Brickley again, as did the vision of his sinking wallet when he recalled the chilling words of the environmental cop: "Where's your dive flag?" *Just not my frappin' morning. Things can only get better!*

Depressed, Brickley glanced toward Tuckernut Beach,

looking for the lifeguard, only to find her already staring at him. "Ship-Shape" Patti Shipley gave him a wave, and his heart skipped several beats. He waved back, trying not to betray the fact that he, a twenty-four-year-old virgin, was hopelessly in love with her since the sixth grade.

Good-looking and powerfully built as he was, Brickley's bashful nature always kicked in around attractive women. "Most Valuable Player" of the Easterly High School football team, he should have had women licking his toes. Painfully shy and tongue-tied around women: That's what he was.

Painfully.

When Brickley did date, he was never at ease. He preferred to follow rather than lead a dance step. He never got involved romantically unless she literally grabbed him and pinned him down. She had to be as aggressive as a linebacker blitzing a quarterback. If Shipley played football, she'd have more sacks than any linebacker in the history of the sport.

Why did he become a summer guard for the village when he went to bed feeling guilty, because he reported a suspicious guy looking in store windows at night? Besides, every other coastal town had "summer constables," with arrest power and everything.

I wouldn't want to arrest anyone, anyway.

How could one so timid have become a much-feared defensive linebacker in the roughest sport in America? Why did he teach fourth graders instead of investigating crimes? After all, his father had been a Providence cop.

Who knows and who cares? thought Brickley.

Flushed with embarrassment, he pulled his eyes away from Patti Shipley's gaze. With great caution, he continued across the slippery rocks and stopped at the end of the jetty to peer into the greenish depths. The visibility at this spot wasn't so bad. Brickley could barely make out the sandy bottom, about eight feet down, where something caught his attention. Something small. A low swell heaved itself lazily against the rocks. The current caused an undulating patch of seaweed to sway, revealing beneath it a whitish object with some kind of movement around it.

Probably some garbage or old bait. Or maybe evidence!

Brickley suddenly heard the padding of bare feet behind him. Before he could turn around, a powerful hand slapped wetly against his back, knocking him forward. There was

A Little Night Fishing

no place in front of him other than a three-foot drop to the uneasy water. Wildly swinging his arms to hold his balance, Brickley felt stabbing pain as fingernails bit into the flesh on the back of his neck as the hand to which they were attached grabbed the neckline of his wet suit and hauled him back to safety. He looked behind him to see Patti Shipley's grinning face one foot away from his. He smelled coconut sunscreen.

"Hi, frogman! How's the Chief of Security this morning?"

"Uh...hi!" Brickley responded as he felt welts rising on the back of his neck. He assumed they were bleeding, and he glanced at Patti's hand to see if there was any of his skin hanging from her perfectly manicured, red fingernails.

"Did I surprise you?"

"Well, uh...yes," Brickley managedto say. "Uh, aren't you supposed to be on the beach?"

Twenty yards from the jetty's end, an eye the size of a baseball poked out of the water and studied the two figures on the rocks. The creature could barely hear their voices, and it listened very carefully.

"What was with the rescue squad and the environmental cop?"

"Oh, uh, somebody reported a diver in distress. They thought it was me."

"Ha!" Patti smiled. "I was following that little drama coming over the walkie-talkie. Why did the environmental patrolman write you a ticket? No diver's flag?"

"Uh...yeah," Brickley admitted with defeat.

"Happens to the best of them. Oh well."

"My pal, Sergeant Fergosi, told me some kid disappeared around here last night. His car is still in the parking lot. Um, they told me to keep an eye out for anything suspicious."

Shipley became serious. "Yeah, Brickley. Me, too. I've already talked to the cops about it. I hope he's okay."

She had always called him "Brickley" instead of "Bob", but there was something cute about the way she did it.

Brickley looked down at his finger, where blood had finally stopped oozing. There was a jagged rip, courtesy of one pissed-off blue crab.

Shipley looked like she wanted to say more. She glanced back toward the beach, where she noticed several swimmers getting into the water. She also saw a man pointing a camera with a telephoto lens directly at her.

"Well, Chief" she said hesitantly, "I guess I should go back. Drop by and visit. It can get a little boring sitting on the beach and being responsible for a bunch of lives all day long!" She grinned.

"Okay," Brickley gushed, his heart quickening.

He watched Shipley hop and leap with tremendous agility over the sharp, slick, uneven rocks leading back to the beach. He found himself relishing the fading sting from her fingernails.

Patti touched me!

Then panic. *Uh oh! What should I talk about? What if I say something really dumb? Just let her do the talking. Yeah, that's it...*

Brickley's self confidence started to ease back in.

* * * *

The short, potbellied, lobster-red photographer snapped another shot of the wet-suited guy poking around at the end of the jetty. Earlier, he'd photographed a hulking thug of a policeman inspecting the spot. Next to the photographer stood a scrawny, greasy man. They were "Flash" Swynecock and his understudy, Lance Grebe, newly arrived in Tuckernut for a vacation, at least officially. Unofficially, Swynecock was always working. A freelance photographer, his prime customers were sleazy, tabloid newspapers and private investigators who needed juicy shots of their clients' spouses misbehaving. Several times, Swynecock had landed handsome fees from "interested parties" for shots of wealthy or influential people in utterly compromising acts. These would be released to the media unless the subjects forked over huge amounts. If necessary, the pictures were even doctored a little. The subjects always paid up.

Business was good.

Swynecock suspected that something was up and regretted leaving his police scanner and video camera in the motel room. For a sleaze paparazzo like Flash Swynecock, there was no such thing as a real vacation, just working vacations, and his working nose told him that opportunity was in the air.

High on Patti Shipley, Brickley returned his attention to the illusive object off the end of the jetty. He eased carefully down the slimy rocks to the waterline, stooped, cupped his hands around his eyes, and strained to see the bottom.

There it was, again! He stood up, glanced toward the lifeguard chair where Shipley watched a small flock of bathers splashing in the low swells, then glanced back at the object. Something about it piqued his attention, and the more he looked, the more curious he became. He knew very well that jumping off the end of the jetty was against the rules and a very good way to earn Shipley's wrath. She usually nailed one or two bathers each summer—idiots who dove off the end only to get pulled under by the eddies swirling just beneath the surface as the currents mixed and flowed at the mouth of the Breachway.

Again, Brickley looked back at Shipley, then at the quivering image of the object below.

Shit! I must be crazy!

With one more nervous glance back toward the lifeguard, he worked the strap of his diving mask over his head. Tightening his weight belt and slipping his flippers back on, he sucked in the deepest breath he could, then slipped into the water. At that moment, the baseball-sized eye that had watched the man talking with the authority figure disappeared quietly beneath the surface. The monster slowly beat its deeply forked tail side to side as it slid toward the jetty.

Brickley was an experienced diver and could hold his breath for a minute or more in calm conditions. Now, he was kicking and stroking like a mad frog, struggling his way toward the sandy bottom. The eight feet seemed like eighty because of those damned currents. A thin mist began to appear on his mask. The outgoing current pushed his legs away from the jetty like wind against a weather vane.

Had Brickley looked seaward with an unfogged mask, he would have noticed a huge shadow hovering nearby. His back was turned to it as he stroked harder, fighting a current that was stronger than he expected. With great effort, he came within reach of the clump of seaweed that swayed around the object. Despite the cold water, his face perspired from the struggle, fogging the mask even more.

Visibility almost vanished. His lungs were starting to burn.

Brickley reached out and pushed the seaweed aside. He could barely make out an undulating mass of crabs. He waved his hands, making some of them scatter. Beneath them was a sneaker. The current tugged at Brickley's feet, and he fought to keep it from pulling him away. Just as he reached for the sneaker, trying to spook two big red crabs that fought over something inside the shoe, an eddy pulled him backward. Much to his surprise, his feet thudded against the bottom, then his rear end. His feet suddenly whipped over his head in a backward somersault.

Air! I need air!

Brickley tried to push himself off the bottom, but it was like being in a hole in the water. He had no buoyancy against the current. Again, he was thrown backward in a somersault, and terror took control. His lungs were about to burst. With his feet planted firmly, Brickley lunged upward and kicked desperately. Suddenly, his right flipper hit something solid and rough—maybe a barnacle-covered rock he hadn't noticed before. He pushed hard off it. All he could think of was getting to the surface.

From the beach, Patti Shipley's sixth sense told her that something was wrong. She noticed that Brickley had disappeared, and it occurred to her that the fool must have jumped in after whatever he'd been looking at. Just then, she saw him blast to the surface in front of the jetty, apparently gasping, then disappear once again.

"Oh, shit!"

The current yanked Brickley back toward the bottom, and by now, he was in complete panic. In his instant at the surface, he'd failed to get all the air he needed. Next thing he knew, his lungs sucked in seawater, and he wracked with spasms. Brickley's hands reached for the quick-release to his weight belt.

Once again, his foot struck the same, rough object. It was moving. Without thinking, he pushed off it and broke the surface, where iron hands gripped his shoulders, spinning him onto his back. His own floundering, clawing hands were out of control as Shipley hauled him out of the currents and toward the beach.

Flash Swynecock's camera snapped away.

A crowd formed and, grateful for some excitement on an otherwise slow morning, he intently watched the lifeguard drag in the muscular, gagging, and black-suited figure. She dragged him onto the beach and straddled him, placed both hands against his stomach and shoved. Water, vomit and a loud, inhuman gushing sound shot out of Brickley's mouth, causing several children who closed in around the spectacle to cringe and shout, "Oooh, gross!" and "Yuck!"

Brickley's eyes fluttered open. The pain from Patti's first assault upon his midsection still wracked him. Then, he glanced down to see her positioning her battering-ram hands on his stomach for another shove. Brickley moved a hand over hers to try to stop it, but it slowed Patti's next thrust as effectively as a pussy willow slowing a locomotive. More seawater and vomit blasted from Brickley's mouth, again accompanied by his inhuman gagging sound.

Again the crowd "yucked" and "grossed," which caused even more kids to shove their way through to see the reason. The clearer Brickley's mind became, the more embarrassed he got, especially when he saw people snapping pictures with their smart phones.

"There's a great band playing tomorrow night at the Titanic Café," Shipley said as she maneuvered her hands for another thrust into Brickley's gut. His protesting hands fell limply against hers. He closed his eyes and braced himself.

Shipley gave a little grunt as her hands plunged into his stomach again, and Brickley's tortured mind pictured his solar plexus biting through his diaphragm, causing internal bleeding and organ damage. To the murmur of the crowd, he spit up less bile this time, his gagging less violent.

"He puked up more the last time," he heard one kid inform a new arrival.

Shipley paid no attention.

"I'd love for you to hear them. Are you free tomorrow night?" she asked.

Brickley forced his eyes open to see a solid wall of faces, both young and old, several with their phones held high, and one potbellied guy with an expensive-looking camera. They were all staring in the same way you'd look at road kill.

"Oh, God!" Then to Shipley, "I think so," as he wiped the vomit from his face.

"I know where the Titanic is!" a small girl shouted proudly, and with a piercing voice. "My big sister is a waitress there! It's the place on the beach that has all those bright lights! You guys are going there tomorrow night? Cool!"

The kid was with her dad—a skinny guy of about forty-five. The man smiled as the crowd chuckled, continuing to stare at Brickley. Something out in the water caught the man's eye, and the smile faded. There was a disturbance about twenty yards offshore. Then, what looked like the tip of a huge shark's tail, headed seaward, broke the surface for just an instant.

For a moment, the man wanted to shout for people to look, but he caught himself just in time.

No way, he thought. *It couldn't be. There are no sharks in these waters!*

His attention was recaptured by Patti Shipley helping Brickley to his feet. People clapped.

* * * *

The crabs, still fighting over the contents of the sneaker, scattered into the rocks as the giant shark inched carefully toward it. As it did so, the monster thought, *Tomorrow night. The "Chief of Security". The place with all the lights. I'll be there.*

In the same way a person might pick up a stranger's well-used handkerchief, the shark gingerly took the very end of the sneaker between two huge teeth, then disappeared into the murk.

Chapter Three

The fog slithered in at dusk like a giant squid, wrapping the shore in its dripping tentacles. Bob Brickley stepped onto West Beach carrying his eleven-foot surf-casting pole, a chair, and a bucket. Inside his backpack were his hooks, lures, fishing line, flashlight, bug repellent, a scaler, and a serrated fishing knife. The fog was so thick that Brickley couldn't see the water from the end of the boardwalk, but he could hear it. The swell had been building since this morning.

This morning! Brickley winced at the thought of his spear-fishing fiasco, nearly drowning, being rescued, and then pummeled by the iron hands of Patti Shipley in front of a sell-out crowd. Not to mention losing his beloved but short-lived spear gun, and his lost belt weights at $70 a pop.

Sore wasn't the word for his lungs and stomach, let alone his pride.

Brickley shook his head vigorously to rid it of the morning's images. He was here to fish and enjoy the quiet for a change. Nothing but. After several unsuccessful nights bottom fishing from the shore with chunks of menhaden, Brickley decided to try something new: live eels. The decision wasn't easy. Brickley had long regarded it as singularly cruel. Impaling a live eel with a barbed hook, then tossing it into the sea to thrash in agony and panic to attract a passing striped bass or bluefish. One method was to hook the poor tyke through its eye sockets.

Yet, live eels were the best way to catch stripers, and Brickley had been skunked all week long. There hadn't even been a nibble by anything but skates, dogfish, and crabs. Still, a sense of guilt clawed at him. It was as if he'd lose his moral virginity as the hook bit into an eel's flesh, as if he'd never again be able to claim that he had compassion for other creatures.

Brickley slogged his way across the soft sand toward his favorite spot, then gratefully dropped his gear. He worked a sand spear into the beach and slid the handle of his pole into it. He turned his attention to the eels, slithering in their own slime at the bottom of a bucket. Again, guilt ran its cold, sharp fingernails up and down his spine. Which one would be the first victim of a death as obscene as any Brickley could think of? He shined his flashlight at the perfectly innocent, snake-like fish and had an idea.

Maybe, I should let them go. I'll just cast with an artificial lure.

Then, as in an old-time cartoon, a little devil popped up on his left shoulder.

You're a fisherman who's had a shitty day, Bob. You deserve some luck, and striped bass is the best eating! Live eels are the best way to catch striped bass!

The gushy wump of a wave snapped Brickley's attention back to the sea. Unlike Tuckernut Beach, which was somewhat sheltered by the jetties guarding the Breachway entrance, West Beach was directly exposed to waves from the open ocean. Grateful for the distraction, he strode toward the line of froth marking the border between land and sea. Wearing his chest-waders, Brickley stood close to the edge as another wave thumped against the beach and immediately wrapped itself around his legs at knee-height. It surged past him, only to pull irresistibly back into the black, gurgling water like a monster's tongue.

Brickley noted the power behind what was not at all a tall wave. Its crest rose barely a foot before breaking, yet there was a lot of water behind it, like a five-foot, eight-inch football player who happened to be 250 pounds of pure muscle. The next wave greedily sucked in the wash of the one before it, then reared up and punched forward against his legs, to sweep well past him.

That was a storm swell, a hell of a lot more powerful than your average wave. Trouble coming.

It was as though a powerful rage was slowly building in the sea. Brickley wondered just how big the waves were going to get.

In fact, a tropical storm system—unusual for this early in the summer—raged about 500 miles south-southeast of where Bob Brickley stood.

Maybe, we'll get it. The body surfing should be awesome tomorrow, and kiss the visibility for spear fishing good-bye, as though I should care!

A Little Night Fishing

The image and the irony of that impaled striper dragging that spear gun into the depths jabbed at him, again. With that, he turned his back to the sea and climbed through the sucking wet sand to his equipment. Standing over his bucket in the gloom, his heart sank again, devil or no devil.

Live eels. Okay, no more procrastinating! Let's do some fishing! Tonight, I'm gonna catch me a big one!

Brickley's heart quickened as he loosened the drag of his reel and pulled the hook and line of his fishing pole down to the bucket. He grabbed a rag to grasp an eel and, with his pocket flashlight in his mouth, directed its beam into the bucket. Six eels lay motionless, their black eyes glistening in the light.

Which one? Okay, the small one.

Brickley reached down and snagged it. It immediately wrapped itself around his arm, its slime oozing as he lifted it from the bucket and braced it against the sand. He grabbed the hook with his other hand and drew it to the head of the clinging eel. His heart pounded, and his mouth became dry. He knew immediately that he couldn't plunge the hook into its eyes. Instead, he decided to punch it through the eel's lower jaw. Wincing, Brickley worked the hook through the eel's skin as a current of horror and guilt surged through him. The tortured fish stiffened, then squirmed wildly. Its tail suddenly shot up Brickley's sleeve, bringing its cold slime with it. It was like, "Take that, Robert Brickley!"

His innocence was lost. The flashlight slipped out of his mouth and hit the sand as he pulled the still-writhing eel off his arm. That was when he noticed the other fisherman. He materialized silently out of the mist, and his huge form stood outlined against the fog, massive in the glow of the lights of the parking lot behind him. Two thoughts immediately popped into Brickley's mind. The first was an odd, primal fear.

Must be the guy's size.

The second thought was, *Why the hell is this guy setting up so close to me when he's got the whole damned beach to fish from?*

Brickley turned his attention back to his fishing pole and the slithering, knotted lump attached to his line. He dropped the slime-covered cloth next to the bucket and stood up, ready to make his first cast. Brickley noticed the looming shadow had moved even closer to him and was watching him with an intensity that sliced through the fog like a knife.

"How's it going?" Brickley called. The figure didn't respond. Brickley's unease increased. Along with his guilt over the eel came another gnawing feeling: Fear.

From time-to-time most fishermen, especially night fishermen, liked to drink. Heavily. Brickley had more than once seen some drunk jerk act like he had more of a right to the beach than anyone else, resulting in a fist-fight with another drunk fisherman with the same attitude. As if on key, Brickley heard the muffle of voices and footsteps coming up the boardwalk.

More fishermen!

Forcing himself to ignore the original intruder, Brickley lifted the pole out of its holder and reeled the squirming bundle at the end of his line up from the sand. He wondered if the poor eel had wrapped itself into a knot around the line. He needed to take another look before he cast. Brickley slid his pole back into its holder, knelt down, and picked up the flashlight. He beamed the light at the eel, and the vision of a stage actor in the spotlight darted absurdly into his mind. Covered with sand and glistening with slime, the eel thrashed wildly. Brickley winced again, then noticed a line of bright red blood running down the eel's body.

Without warning, the enormous figure burst forward. Brickley yelped and fell backward as the giant lunged directly for the hapless eel. Brickley gazed with stark horror at a scene from a sick nightmare. The intruder's head, and especially its jaws, were huge. Inhumanly huge. The remaining light caught the creature the instant its jaws closed around the squirming eel with a gunshot-like snap. The monster leaped into the air, swung its head wildly from side-to-side, then jumped high into the air again like a fighting sailfish. Suddenly, it darted toward the water. Brickley's pole bent forward, and the reel screamed as the monster plunged into the ocean.

The damned thing was hooked!

The reel hissed so loudly that it caught the attention of the newly arrived fishermen, who came running.

"Wow!" cried a middle-aged, potbellied local who reeked of alcohol.

"Holy shit!" shouted another.

"I've never seen a reel get stripped like that!"

Brickley sat dumbly on the sand, his blood frozen, his mouth unable to close.

A Little Night Fishing

The hissing suddenly stopped.

"Set the hook now, man!" shouted the potbellied guy. Brickley's mouth began flapping, yet no words would come.

"Now, or you'll lose it!"

Brickley couldn't move.

The new intruders came to the quick conclusion that the guy was a rank beginner who had no idea how to fish. Without a word, Potbelly yanked Brickley's pole from the holder, set the drag on the reel, and, to Brickley's horror, slammed the pole back.

"Yeah! Got 'im!" Potbelly cried as the pole lurched forward. He loosened the drag again, and the line flew screaming off the reel. "This is the biggest fish I've ever had on a line! Hahaha!"

Brickley struggled to speak. The best he could manage was a spasm-like groan.

The hissing of the reel stopped abruptly. Again, Potbelly tightened the drag and began to reel the line in. There was no tension at all. The fisherman knew the line hadn't snapped.

"He's making a run back toward the beach!" he cried as he cranked the reel.

Oh...my...God! Brickley's mind cried.

"You don't know what you're doing!" Brickley finally blurted to the ecstatic fisherman.

"I don't! Look who's talking!" Potbelly shot back without trying to hide his contempt. He furiously reeled in the line. "Yep," he shouted to his cronies, "it's still making a run to the beach!"

"Let it go!" Brickley hollered frantically, finally rising to his feet. "Run!"

"You're crazy!" retorted Potbelly.

"You don't understand!"

"No, *you* don't understand!" the fisherman shot back. His buddies laughed in a not-very-good-natured way, then began cheering on their pal.

"You got 'im, Jack!"

"Way to go, Jack!"

"Reel that sucker in!"

Brickley bent down to pick up his flashlight, but it wasn't there. He desperately clawed at the sand for the light, but with no luck. He plunged his hands into his knapsack, searching for his knife. He yelped as a fish hook bit deeply into his finger, but his yelp was drowned out by the moron's ecstatic laughter as the pole again slammed forward, and the line began tearing off the reel.

Brickley's hands finally grasped the knife handle. He yanked it out of its sheath and lunged toward the screeching, jerking rod. With one quick slash, the tension on the pole ceased, and the reel fell silent. Gasping for air, Brickley slumped to the sand, his hand bleeding from the deeply impaled hook.

Everyone was motionless as the shocked, dumbfounded drunk held the pole. He finally screamed, "You goddamned shithead! Do you know what you've done?"

Brickley ran for all he was worth.

Chapter Four

Bob Brickley's eyes were wild and unfocused. He sat erect on the edge of a chair in his apartment, staring at nothing. All he could see was the image of the giant fisherman with the shark's head. All he could hear was the sickening snap of its jaws as it took eel, hook, line, and all. Brickley's eyes closed, and he grimaced as he tried to make some sense—any sense—of this.

Perhaps it's some sort of survival mechanism. The human mind always takes what it experiences and makes it fit the nearest possible explanation that it can understand. Some call it "denial".

Some sick guy in a shark suit? Brickley asked—pleaded with himself.

If that's a suit, it beats the hell out of anything Hollywood can deliver.

No way.

His hands drew into fists as something primal in him tightened. With a gasp, Brickley realized that Nature, God, Satan, Something, had just chewed up the world as we understand it and spit it out. Nothing for Bob Brickley would ever be the same, again. Then, another thought hit him like a slap in the face.

Are there more of them?

He shot out of the chair and gulped for air as he remembered the missing fisherman.

Oh, my God! The kid was murdered, and I've just met his murderer! Oh God! Oh God! What do I do? Nobody will believe me! I wouldn't believe me!

Then, Brickley's mind raced back to what he had just witnessed, and he became utterly certain that he had met Ralph Hunley's killer.

What kind of death did that poor kid go through?

Brickley remembered the sneaker covered with ravenous crabs, and he realized why the crabs were all over it. He felt sick to his stomach.

What do I do? What do I do? What do I do?

* * * *

An hour after Brickley had fled West Beach, the three intoxicated fishermen sat silently in their beach chairs. "The asshole" left all his bait and gear behind, so Jack and his buddies simply appropriated it. Their poles rose from their sand spears, lines arching into the ocean and baited with desperately struggling live eels hooked through their eye sockets. Their yellow rain slickers dripped as the fog grew even thicker. All was silent except for the regular wumping of waves against the shore, but the wall of fog was so heavy that it even muffled that sound.

Animated banter about their encounter with "the asshole" and what would easily have been the biggest fish ever caught from a beach anywhere in New England had wound down. Because of "the asshole", Jack missed being a celebrity fisherman with his name in the record books. His picture would have made the cover of every sport fishing magazine in the country. The news would have interviewed him. He'd have offers coming in from publishers and fishing programs, a chance to star in his own fishing video.

They all agreed that it wasn't a giant bluefish or striper. It weighed at least 200 pounds, probably more. It must be something like a tuna. Jack would have been the first guy ever to catch a tuna from the shores of this state. Jack burned off his rage by guzzling whiskey and firing off salvo after salvo of powerful and creative cuss-word combinations, all colorfully suggesting his feelings about the beginner-idiot. His friends fully agreed, discussing at length what they would do to the big twit if he came back on the beach to fetch his gear. Phrases such as, "kick his ass" and "beat the living shit out of him" flowed freely, and they meant it.

They finally fell silent, fatigued by the haze of alcohol and the late hour. Their hopes of re-hooking that glorious fish were fading. Their lines had been still all night.

Then, it happened.

It was Jack's—formerly Bob Brickley's—pole that lurched forward. In a flash, Jack bolted from his chair and grabbed the pole from the holder. He clutched it like a child as his eyes gleefully watched the line screaming off the reel. It was another big one! It had to be!

Jack's buddies were on their feet, watching with their breaths held, waiting for the line to stop—waiting for that crucial, delicate moment when a fisherman feels in his gut that it's time to set the drag and slam the pole back to set the hook.

Oh please, oh please! they all thought.

The thrill of watching another pulling in a fish was almost as exciting as being the one with the pole. The reel suddenly went quiet. Jack knew that the fish was starting to swallow the bait.

Now!

With trembling hands, he tightened the drag, then yanked backward violently. With adrenaline taking control, the yank was more violent than he intended, but the line didn't snap. In fact, Jack screamed a war-howl as the pole slammed forward under the renewed pull of the great fish.

"It's him! It's him!" screamed Jack. "Ahaha! I've got 'im!" He practically sobbed with joy. He loosened the drag again as it became instantly clear that his twenty-pound test line could easily snap from the weight of this incredible fish.

Let's tire out that beautiful bastard, then start to work it in.

This was going to be a long fight, and Jack and his pals were ready.

"You got 'im, Jack!"

"Steady, Jack. Steady!"

"Yeah! Yeah! Yeah!"

In one shocking instant, the reel stopped, and the tension on the pole disappeared. A shudder of dread that Jack had lost the fish rippled through all three men.

"No...no... Not again!"

Jack tightened the drag and began reeling in the line, cautiously at first, then with greater speed.

"Did you lose it?"

"I don't fuckin' know!" Jack growled. Suddenly, he howled with relief as his pole doubled over, again.

"Yes! Yes! He's still on! He was just making a run toward shore! Hahaha!"

Then the reel went silent yet again.

"You're not going to fool me this time, beautiful! He's running for shore!"

Jack cranked the reel as quickly as he could to haul in the

limp line. He readied himself for the colossal fish to make another dash back to sea, but it wasn't happening.

"He's still coming toward us!" Jack gasped with awe as he cranked in the line. "He's still coming toward us!" He reeled faster. "I might be landing this thing sooner than I thought, if the stupid bastard doesn't decide to land itself! It's still coming at us!" Jack was incredulous.

His pals ran toward the break, peering into the fog as the waves grabbed at their legs. They could see the swells emerge from the fog just moments before they peaked and tumbled, which was a little disconcerting, and both were surprised at the power of the backwash. They had to resist its force and reset their weight as the sand under their feet shifted, the water trying to suck them into the black void. They listened intently for the sloshing of the great fish breaking the surface as Jack pulled it into shallow water. They heard nothing but the sound of the waves.

"Is he still coming in?" one man asked.

"Yeah, I guess so," Jack replied, doubt gnawing its way back into him. "He's gotta' be."

Suddenly, Jack shouted, "Yeah! He's still on!"

The three men gazed intently toward the sea, then heard the sound of the surface break.

"I hear it! I hear it! He sounds big!"

"Hold 'er steady, Jack!"

Then, they finally saw it. They didn't try to speak, because they had no idea what to say. They began backing up as the shadow of a huge man emerged from the breakers, his hand firmly grasping the end of Jack's line and coiling it between his hand and his elbow. In the parking lot-glow of the fog, both men saw his teeth glisten.

"So, the purpose of this hook is to 'catch' me, I take it," the shadow spoke with a heart-stopping, sloshing growl to the three anglers.

Hearing the inhuman voice and with pole still in hand, Jack moved toward his buddies, then stopped in his tracks. The three men stood gaping at the enormous figure looming over them. It held Jack's hook in his hand, and then thrust it at his face.

"I believe this is yours." Its wet, guttural voice was right out of a horror movie.

"Oh, shit," Jack gasped, his eyes unable to tear themselves away from this...this what?

A Little Night Fishing

Spasms of terror and disbelief shot through each of them as the creature's head suddenly expanded, its neck transforming into a glistening, white continuation of the torso of what was becoming a giant shark with legs and arms. Its gaping jaws suddenly filled with jagged rows of flashing, serrated teeth.

In a split second, the monster's arms shot out. Still holding the hook and line attached to Jack's pole, its enormous fists smashed brutally against the foreheads of the other two men. They crumbled to the wet sand just in time for a wave to wash over them. Still gaping and dropping the pole, Jack backed away as the creature moved toward him.

"Aw, now. Why did you do that?" the thing croaked. "The reel's gonna get sand in it. Naughty boy!"

Jack came to his senses long enough to try and run, but years of neglecting his body, not to mention too much alcohol, made his movements anything but agile. An iron hand grabbed his shoulder and flung him around. With a cry, Jack spun backward onto the beach, breathing in quick gasps as the hideous figure loomed over him.

"I hope you enjoyed catching me!" it ululated sarcastically and hatefully.

"No...No...I'm sorry! Please!" Jack crab-walked backward, away from the creature.

"Do unto others as you would have others do unto you, right?"

"Oh..."

The monster reached down, gripped Jack's collar, and hoisted him high into the air. He held Jack's face inches from his own. Jack screamed, then gagged as the thing's heavy, rotten, fish-odor breath assaulted him. The creature held the hook in front of Jack's face.

"Your turn, now!" it said with glee. "Are you ready?"

With a lightning-fast jab, the creature punched Jack in the face and the man flew backward, landing with a grunt on the beach. The creature fell on him. Jack tried to scream but only gagged as the monster thrust its hand into Jack's mouth. It pulled down the man's jaw until it dislocated with a sickening snap. Its other hand held the heavily barbed hook. Jack had no trouble screaming grotesquely in agony when the monster thrust the hook deeply into the roof of his mouth.

It stood and snatched up the pole while Jack clawed

madly at the hook embedded in his pallet. The monster heard a sound behind it, and it turned to receive a desperate body-block from one of Jack's half-crazed friends. For the man, it was like running into a wall.

Amused by this rash and feeble effort, the thing grabbed the man's face in a huge hand and jerked it back. The snapping of the man's neck came through crystal clear, and he was dead before he hit the sand. The monster sensed movement to its left and turned in time to see the other man lunging at him with a knife. A quick front-kick to the stomach with its massive left leg stopped the man cold. Then, the creature placed its left pinkie on the man's forehead and gently pushed back. He landed in a heap on the beach. Still holding the fishing pole, it stooped and picked the man up by the seat of his pants.

"Hey, watch this!" it called to Jack with sarcastic joy. Displaying unearthly strength, it lifted the hapless angler with one arm and held him dangling over its gaping maw. The mouth yawned open, jaws dislocating just like those of a great white shark. The man shrieked in a pitch so high that it was almost unrecognizable as human. The creature dangled the victim over its mouth, just to hear him scream a little longer before silencing him forever.

Jack lay crumpled in a bloody pile, moaning, sobbing, disbelieving. His glazed eyes glued in horror to the ungodly spectacle of his screaming friend being lowered into this shark-man's mouth like a bunch of grapes. First, the man's head disappeared between the murderous jaws, into the thing's torpedo-like body. Instantly, the screaming became muffled, then stopped altogether. The monster's head arched upward, and its neck and chest lurched up and down in violent, electrified spasms. Its gullet muscles rippled with a force that would suck down a horse.

Jack watched in stunned fascination as, soon, only his friend's feet jutted from the creature's mouth. The monster's stomach bulged and squirmed as the swallowed fisherman's grisly struggles continued unbelievably, and Jack knew that his friend was still alive. Then, the undulating lump in the monster's belly gave one last violent thrash as those bone-cutter jaws chomped shut, and two bloody, flip-flop shod feet plopped to the sand.

The thing turned to Jack, held open its massive hands,

and said, "All gone!" in its distorted rumble. It then patted its bulging, heaving stomach and said, "Boy, I'm stuffed!" Then, it called out, "I can't believe I ate the whole thing!" It croaked a parody of a laugh.

Jack wretched, then vomited.

"Yuck!" burbled the monster. "Crummy in the tummy?" it mocked.

It moved toward Jack and whispered in its devil-voice, "Now, how about a little sport fishing?"

Jack sobbed anew as he slowly inched backward. Blood poured down Jack's throat from the impaling fishhook and his dangling lower jaw.

"Isn't that what it's all about—the *sport* of it?"

"...aleaze!" Jack tried to gag through blood, hook, missing jaw, and indescribable agony.

"I beg your pardon?"

"Aleaze...on't!" Every syllable was a torment.

"Are you begging for mercy?"

"Ah...es...ahh!"

"Just like the mercy you showed those eels you were fishing with—jamming a hook through their eye sockets while the things were still alive?"

Jack's body wracked with pain, sobs, and utter despair.

"Okay, I'll let you go this time." The creature reached back to Jack's battered face and, with a violent tug, jerked the hook out, taking with it most of the roof of the man's mouth.

"On second thought, why don't I try your method?" The shark-man-thing knelt on Jack's shoulders and held his face steady with a vise-like grip. With its other hand, it held the large, barbed hook in front of Jack's eyes.

"Do you see this?"

With a lightning-fast stroke, the monster buried the hook in Jack's left eye, worked it through the bone to the man's bubbling shriek, then worked it through his other eye socket. The barbed end of the hook popped out of Jack's tear duct.

"And now, a little *sport*!"

It grabbed Jack by the collar and lifted him to his feet.

"Run!" it rumbled.

Now in shock, blind, and completely disoriented but somehow still conscious, Jack stumbled dumbly toward the boardwalk, his hands clawing around the hook as the jelly from his eyeballs mixed with blood, oozing down his cheeks. The thing loosened the drag, and as the line fed slowly off the reel, it constructed a mock dialogue between two people.

"I've got one!" it taunted. "Steady, Jack, steady!" it teased. "Yeah! It's a big one! It's too big to be a striper or a bluefish! It's gotta be a tuna! Or a human! Ahahaha!"

Its demon-voice rose.

"I hope it's a human! They make the greatest faces when they get hooked! They make hysterical noises, too! Ahaha! Ahahaha!"

Jack tumbled sightlessly over a pile of seaweed, and the play of the reel stopped.

"It's swallowing the bait, now," the creature bellowed. "Time to set the hook!"

The creature slammed back the pole, and Jack gagged, trying to move a jaw that wouldn't work. He couldn't even scream, anymore. With a last burst of primal strength and determination, he scrambled to his feet and ran. The reel sang.

"You got 'im, Jack! Steady, Jack! Yeah! Yeah! Yeah! Is he still on? I don't know!" the thing boomed.

It jerked the pole again, snapping Jack's head backward. He hit the ground with a wet thud.

The monster cranked in the line, guffawing at the sight of this wretched, broken human mass staggering, mouth first, toward it.

"Gee, did I lose him? Or is he making a run toward shore? Yes—yes! He's still on! He must be making a run for shore! Get ready to land it—if the stupid thing doesn't try to land itself! Ahahahahahaha!"

Then, knowing that he was about to pass out, the night fisherman-turned-fish did the bravest thing he had ever done in his wretched life. He charged this unreal devil, only able to guess the location and distance. Jack guessed well, but before he could collide with this aberration of nature, the thing straight-armed him right in what was left of his face. Jack latched on to the arm with its thick, sandpaper skin. He tried to yank the arm behind the creature in a futile effort to break it, but for amusement, the shark let him wrap its arm around its shark-like body with the flexibility of rubber.

"Cartilage," the creature said in mock apology. It dropped the fishing pole, shook its arm loose, and firmly grasped Jack by his shoulders. It stared into his dripping eye sockets.

"Do you want to give me a hug? I guess I've got one of those sensitive men who needs positive reinforcement in order to keep feeling good about himself," he said, his fetid breath assaulting Jack's tattered senses anew. "No offense, Bud, but I'm getting sick of you."

The shark-man yanked the hook from what was left of Jack's eye sockets, then took his entire head easily into its cavernous mouth, biting down with that nauseating snap. With a ghastly snapping of bones, Jack's headless body fell to the sand, blood spurting from his jagged neck. The creature swallowed the head with a loud gulp.

Looking down at what was left of Jack, it then glanced at the crumpled figure of the other dead fisherman. The thing patted its grossly extended stomach and said out loud, "I really am stuffed. I guess these two guys are leftovers, and I have a few friends who just *love* leftovers."

Chapter Five

The human mind can't always deal with its more fringe experiences, because it functions within a certain relatively comfortable frame of reference. When the five senses feed the mind information that's outside that frame of reference—like being in a serious accident, experiencing combat, or meeting ravenous shark-men—the mind can shut down for a time. What it usually does is find a way to make the experience fit that comfortable frame of reference, and that's what Bob Brickley's mind did.

Terrified, disbelieving, and with the thought that he was going nuts, Brickley planned to call in sick the next day. Though, he didn't want to be alone with thoughts of the horror he'd witnessed. He had to get a grip. There was only one explanation.

There's no way that wasn't a maniac in a costume. That's not reassuring, though. There's a maniac out there, and he might have killed that Hunley kid!

The next morning at 8:00 a.m., Brickley struggled into his security guard uniform and slogged into work, picking up his portable two-way radio and an unmarked Jeep at the Tuckernut substation of the Easterly Police Department. He knew he needed to report the previous night's incident, but he was already a big joke around here.

If I tell them there's a seven-foot guy running around in a shark suit attacking fishermen, they'll hear the hoots all the way to Providence. What the hell would Holmes do?

The answer to that was easy.

Find the logical explanation, like in 'The Hound of the Baskervilles'.

Soon, Brickley was in broad daylight, dealing with another kind of monster.

"Oh, yeah? What're ya gonna do if I won't move?" The out-of-state tourist, every bit as big as Brickley, folded his arms tightly across his chest. Obviously tipsy, even though it was only 10:00 a.m., he glared defiantly. His out-of-state car with its out-of-state license plates sat on the shoulder of the seaside road at the edge of Tuckernut Village, right in front of a "No Parking" sign. Behind the sign, his out-of-state babe, her jaws pounding a piece of gum, sneered at the security guard from the top of a tall rock.

I hate this job! I hate it! I hate it! thought Brickley as he reached with a shaking hand for his two-way radio.

Town authorities said that his very presence was supposed to be a "deterrent" when the actual cops had better things to do. He'd hate to see how un-seriously people would take him if he were the proverbial ninety-eight-pound weakling.

"I'll have to call the regular police, sir. You'll get a ticket and be asked to take a Breathalyzer test."

"Yeah? You can just take that radio and shove it up your puckered little asshole!"

The tourist glanced at the girl, but she was starting to look a little worried.

"Hey, Leon. Maybe we should just move," she called down from her perch.

"Fuck that!"

He turned back to Brickley, "Hah!"

With an expression of fatigue, Brickley shook his head and stepped back, right into the path of an oncoming car. A horn blasted and Brickley leaped forward, colliding head-on with the tourist, who fell backward with drama worthy of an action movie.

"Assault! I've been assaulted!" he cried, pointing at Brickley. A torrent of foul language poured from him and the girl, until they both stiffened.

Brickley followed their gaze to find a police cruiser slowly trundling to a stop behind their parked vehicles. Brickley groaned. If he was to get help from a "higher power", as Brickley thought of the regular police force then, of all cops, why Sergeant Moron?

Al Fergosi opened the door and stepped slowly out. The abundant police paraphernalia strapped to his chest and belt clanked and jingled on his six-foot, four-inch, 250-pound frame. The expression behind his reflecting sunglasses was blank, with a hint of humorous contempt as he swaggered toward the suddenly compliant tourists.

"What's the trouble?" Fergosi droned officially.

"Nothing, Sergeant. This guard was pointing out that we

couldn't park here, and we were just leaving. Weren't we, babe?"

The woman nodded her head vigorously. Leaping down from the rock, she swooped into the car just in time as the guy pulled away from the curb. Brickley and Fergosi watched the car putting as much distance between it and them as possible without exceeding the speed limit. Brickley finally looked at Fergosi, who was already looking at Brickley. The cop smiled smugly and spread his arms widely.

"I guess some people have it, and others, well..." he shook his head with mock disappointment. "So, why do you work as a rent-a-cop in the summer, anyway? You teachers must not need to work in the summer. Why not just lie on the beach? No offense, Brickley, but you just don't have the..." Fergosi tried not to grin as he searched for the right word, "...presence for any kind of law enforcement."

Brickley just stared down the road, unresponsive. So, Fergosi tried, again.

"Now, I'd like you to do something. Are you listening?"

"Yeah," Brickley said guardedly.

"I'm going to haul-ass up the road until I get to the overlook. Then, I'm going to hit the brakes hard, jump out of the cruiser with my binoculars, and start glaring seaward. You're to arrive in the same way thirty seconds after me, then leap out of your..." He grinned. "...er...security vehicle, also with your binoculars. I'll point, and you'll look. Don't say anything to anybody who asks what's up. Got it?"

Brickley grimaced, but he knew he had less to lose by going along with this, whatever it was.

"Okay."

Guess what happened to me last night, Fergosi?

Brickley watched the cruiser pull away. With any luck, any luck at all, his brakes would fail, and he'd keep going—*off* the overlook. As instructed, Brickley jumped into his unmarked vehicle and sped toward the overlook, coming to an abrupt halt when he got there.

Fergosi stood next to the cruiser, the door still open, peering intently out to sea through his binoculars. Across the street, several pedestrians had stopped and were looking at the sergeant, then toward the horizon, with curiosity. Brickley got out of the Jeep with greater alacrity than usual, walked briskly to Fergosi, who pointed without lowering his binoculars. Brickley brought his own binoculars to his eyes and stared at nothing but open sea. Out of the corner of his eye, he saw Fergosi pull up his two-way radio microphone and start chattering incoherences. He didn't press the button.

This is weird, but so's Sergeant Moron, Brickley thought.

"How many people are gawking?" he asked Brickley.

"Five."

"I'll bet you five bucks that in five minutes we'll have five more," Fergosi replied in a clipped, even voice while pretending to speak into the radio.

"Huh?"

"You heard me. Five bucks says there'll be five more for a total of ten spectators, all of 'em tourists."

Brickley looked at Fergosi and noticed that the huge cop was fighting the urge to grin. He managed to keep a serious, professional expression on his face.

"Okay," said Brickley.

"When I say 'go', we'll both look at our watches. Ready? Go!"

Both men raised their wrists to their faces, then brought the binoculars immediately back to their eyes.

"I've got ten hours and twenty-five minutes," Fergosi asserted.

"I have twenty-five minutes past ten," answered Brickley.

"We'll go by my watch. Now, you point in the direction we're looking."

Brickley pointed, feeling like he was becoming Sergeant Moron Junior.

"Good," Fergosi piped.

As if on cue, a large, sleek, jet-black cigarette boat emerged from around The Point, its raked bow pounding the sea and kicking up vast clouds of spray, its engine roaring mightily while its two wet suit-clad occupants held on.

"Ah, what timing! There goes *Shot Baker*, probably the fastest boat of its size on this shore," Fergosi beamed as though he were an announcer at a sporting event.

"*Shot Baker?*"

"Yep. Named after the atomic bomb test at Bikini Atoll in 1945. You've probably seen footage of it: A nuclear water blast among a fleet of anchored ships. Totally amazing explosion."

Brickley dropped his binoculars and looked at Fergosi. "Actually, it was *'Baker Shot,'* not *'Shot Baker'.* And it was 1946."

Fergosi ignored him.

"You know why they call 'em cigarette boats, Brickley? Because they're so fast and so durable in any weather, they were first used to smuggle cigarettes in from Canada. The Coast Guard couldn't catch 'em!"

Brickley rolled his eyes and looked back toward the hurtling craft. "Who owns the boat?"

"Some summer tourist-types, I'll bet. I just saw it for the first time as it was heading out the Breachway the other day and read its name off the transom. Pretty impressive."

"So, all this bullshit was so people could look at us looking at this boat?"

"But a hell of a nice boat, eh, Brickley?"

After another two minutes, Fergosi told Brickley to count spectators. There were seven, with just under three minutes to go on their bet. Two more spectators approached from down the sidewalk, one of them snapping pictures. The potbellied guy somehow looked familiar to Brickley.

Fergosi's radio crackled to life.

"Six-Nine."

"Six-Nine, go ahead."

"Be advised we have three 10-57s. West Beach. Last night."

Brickley felt like a lightning bolt shoot through him. "Three 10-57s" meant three missing people. At West Beach. The blood drained from his face.

God almighty! Not again!

Brickley jumped as the dispatcher's voice hissed the descriptions of three men. Three night fishermen, and two vehicles—a car and a pickup truck. They were the very vehicles Brickley had almost run into in the West Beach parking lot as he'd fled that mad scene the night before.

"What the hell's the matter with you?" Fergosi was eying him curiously.

"Tell you later."

Brickley tailgated Fergosi's police car to West Beach. His Jeep nearly slammed into the cruiser when Fergosi stopped to let a family of beach-goers with about fifty kids cross the street toward the boardwalk. As both vehicles entered the now-crowded West Beach parking lot, Brickley had no trouble spotting the two vehicles in question.

"Oh, my God!" Brickley uttered. He started to shake.

It really was a killer! My God, I'm a witness to multiple murders!

He watched Fergosi strut toward the parked vehicles and realized he had to tell him. If he waited any longer, they might charge him as an accessory after the fact. He leaped out of the Jeep and ran up to Fergosi, who was peering through a window of the pickup truck.

"I was here last night," he blurted.

Fergosi looked up. "What?"

"I said I was here last night."

For a second, the cop didn't know what to say. Then, "What the hell were you doing here?"

"Fishing." Brickley was trembling, his voice shaky. Fergosi noticed. Something told him not to turn this into a joke.

"Did you see these guys?"

"Yes, I did."

Fergosi couldn't help himself. He turned to Brickley, took off his sunglasses, and gazed seriously into his eyes. "Did you kill them?"

"This is no joke, Fergosi!" Brickley shouted. Two young boys passing by turned to look at them.

"Okay, okay!" Fergosi backed off, repressing a smile. "Did you see anything unusual?"

Here goes, Brickley thought with dread.

"Yes."

"It was foggy as hell last night. How could you see shit?"

"Because I was with the three guys."

"What? All right, spill it, Brickley!"

"This way," said Brickley as he led Fergosi toward the busy but not crowded boardwalk.

"It was foggy as hell, but it happened right about there, where those people are." Brickley pointed to a spot near the water's edge.

They stepped off the boardwalk. Fergosi had his sunglasses back on and looked formidable.

"Folks, could you please leave this area," he called to a group of curious bathers stretched out under beach umbrellas.

From the looks of the big cop, they knew enough not to ask why.

"Please wait by the boardwalk. I have some questions."

"What's this about, Sergeant?" one plucked up the courage to ask.

Fergosi ignored him as he turned back to Brickley, who was already nosing around in the shifting sands.

How the hell do you find any footprints on a beach? Brickley thought. *No holes where the sand spears would have been, either. Even Holmes would be stumped! There could be traces of blood, and where's the fishing tackle I left here?*

"So?" Fergosi's sharp question jolted Brickley out of his detective mode.

"I was fishing here by myself when those three guys showed up. After what happened, I left my stuff here and ran!"

"Ran from what?" Fergosi looked intently at Brickley. "Keep your shit out of your pants and answer the question!"

"Maybe you should ask those people if they saw my stuff when they got here this morning," Brickley whimpered.

Fergosi snorted, then stalked over the boardwalk. By this time, everyone on the beach was staring.

While Fergosi interrogated the vacationers, Brickley's gaze scanned the sand. He spotted holes where kids had been digging, the probable marks of beach chairs and umbrellas—but not a sign of his, or anyone else's, fishing gear.

Fergosi marched back. "They didn't see anything when they got here."

Then, Brickley spotted it. "There!"

It was a darker patch of sand, above the tideline and about ten feet from where they stood. It was big, and even though the average beachgoer would think it was just a wet patch, Brickley and Fergosi knew what it was.

"Shit!" Fergosi muttered, grabbing his mic. "Base, six-nine."

"Base."

"Be advised possible multiple 187s at West Beach last night. Evidence found. 10-49 a team to secure the scene."

Every muscle in Brickley's body tightened.

He's talking about possible multiple killings. I'm in it, now!

The radio sputtered, again.

"Six-nine, base. Did you say 187s?"

"That's affirm. Let's move it! Six-nine out."

He turned back to Brickley. There was no humor in his voice, now. "This is blood. And I sure as hell doubt all this came from a fish. Three possible homicides!"

Try four, Brickley thought with a chill.

"This could be big." Fergosi breathed in. Then, he thrust a meat-hook hand at Brickley. "I don't even want to know what you saw here last night. We need to get back to the station, so you can tell the big boys what you saw—and what you're so damned scared of."

Fergosi eased off.

"Meanwhile, Brickley, your only job is to keep everybody out of this area until we seal it off."

Fergosi turned to walk back to his cruiser, but the rapid clicking of an expensive camera shutter caught his attention. There was a potbellied photographer targeting them from just up the beach.

"Sir, you have to keep clear of this area!"

"Is there a problem, Sergeant?" Flash Swynecock inquired.

"Just follow my directions." Fergosi immediately detested him.

Brickley's eyes returned to the churned-up sand, and he moved from gouge-to-gouge, imagining what horrors might have taken place after he fled.

If I'd stayed here, I might have been a victim, too!

Then, Brickley's heart leaped as he noticed two parallel grooves coming down from the high-water zone. They seem to have escaped the general trampling of beach-goers this morning. They faded out at the tideline, where the waves had washed the sand flat and featureless. Immediately, he pictured an unconscious, or dead, victim dragged into the ocean. A cold wind blew through him.

Brickley glanced toward the boardwalk, and one of the young women standing there reminded him of Patti Shipley.

I wonder if all this will eat into my night with Patti? God, what if they think I'm a suspect?

Brickley's stomach did a somersault as it dawned on him that, on top of all this other trouble, tonight was his first date with Patti the Great!

His stomach was still sore from her pummeling the day before.

What kind of pummeling will I get from the detectives at the station?

Brickley watched a wave roll toward shore, well up, and then topple onto the beach. He noticed that the swell was almost a foot higher than it had been the night before. The newspaper said the tropical storm was 400 miles away and was picking up both strength and speed...and headed in the general direction of New England.

Chapter Six

Detective Rick Angell of the Rhode Island State Police smiled across the desk at Bob Brickley. A local detective whose name Bob had never learned stood leaning against the wall.

"Okay, Bob," Angell said reassuringly. "Relax, take a breath, and tell us what you saw last night."

Bob relaxed, took a breath, and began. The story wasn't long. When he finished, Angell leaned back in his chair and stared at him.

"So, you were surf casting by yourself at about nine. Then, this big guy in a really realistic shark suit shows up, eats the eel right off your line, and runs into the water."

Bob began to flush.

"That's right."

God, do I sound stupid!

"You're sure there was nobody else on the beach at the time? Nobody else saw this guy?"

"No, it was just me."

I'll lose my job. They'll put me away. God, I'll be a suspect!

"Then, these three rowdy guys joined you. You hooked something big. They freaked because you weren't doing it right, and they took over your fishing rod. You thought it might be the nut in the shark suit at the other end of the line, so you cut the line and ran for it."

Brickley felt like a complete idiot.

"That's about it." Then, he rallied and looked at Angell. "I'm just trying to be honest! I'm telling you exactly what I saw!"

"Why didn't you call in about this shark guy last night when you got home? You didn't even report it this morning, and you work right out of the Tuckernut substation."

Brickley shrugged helplessly.

"Easy, Bob. The fact is that you never saw any crime at all. This guy you saw was a wacko, but you didn't see him commit any crime. You left the three guys on the beach, and they were fine."

A Little Night Fishing

"Yes."

"So, you had nothing to report except that you saw three fishermen, and you didn't find out they were missing until this morning."

"Yes." Brickley perked up a bit.

"As a matter of fact, these guys aren't senile or anything. So, they really haven't been missing long enough to even be considered officially missing. The only evidence of anything was that blood on the beach, which could have come from a fish."

"That's right," Bob perked up even more.

"So, our main concern at this point is your report of the shark guy."

"Yes," Brickley replied. "We should be on the lookout for this guy. I'd definitely say he's dangerous."

"Right. You can go, Bob, but don't go too far. We might need you, again," Angell said, standing up. They shook hands, and Brickley left.

The two detectives looked at each other.

"Well, what do you think?" the local detective asked.

"Not too bright. Guy in a shark suit!" Angell scoffed. "The fact is, we don't even know if there's been a crime. Surf was heavy last night. Brickley said those guys were plastered. They might have drowned, and I've seen middle aged guys stage something like this to take off on their wives."

"All three of them?"

"Well, we'll know soon enough. The lab has those blood samples from the beach—if it is blood. The boats are out searching for these guys and for Hunley, and there are APBs out all over the Northeast. Four people missing from a place like Tuckernut in two days." Angell said. Then, he turned to his comrade. "Of course, there's another possibility. Maybe Brickley was plastered, and if there was a killer, maybe it was him."

They look silently at each other.

"Still, this Brickley's not telling us everything. Let's keep an eye on him," Angell said.

* * * *

That evening after work, Brickley drove toward the Titanic Café for his first date with Patti Shipley. He'd been embarrassed enough for one day. He refused to think of making a fool of himself on his first rendezvous with his dream girl. Beethoven-loving Bob's heart fluttered with unease as he spotted the long, loud line of unruly partiers at the doors of the Titanic—a major nightlife hotspot whose brightly lighted rear deck opened directly onto the beach—the thump of waves audible above the din of the crowd. The smell of sea, sand, and that day's sunblock would have been powerful at this time of night but for the fact that these people were all trying to get their smokes in before going inside.

In the crowd were scatterings of multicolored Mohawks, shaved heads, and flowing, teased, tumbling, bleached-blonde hair of the heavy-metal style. Brickley assumed that at least half these people were under-age but would get into the bar, anyway. There was no sign of Shipley. Then, he noticed the marquee looming above the doors: "An Evening with The Reckless Defectors."

Brickley groaned. He checked to make sure his smart phone was still on his belt and half-wished he'd get called in to work, tonight. He took his place at the end of the line, hoping to save a spot for Shipley, and started choking on the smoke. While the mob inched forward, Brickley collected his thoughts and envisioned a general plan for the evening. He'd start by admitting to Shipley that the whole episode with the screaming emergency vehicles was the indirect result of an attack by a crazed blue crab when spearfishing that morning. She'd get a kick out of that.

Then, I'll tell her about the four disappearances! Wow!

He'd save that one for later in the evening, after a few dances. He imagined himself gently swaying cheek to cheek with Shipley. He'd pull her onto the dance floor on the very first slow song, to show her that he was a man of action! Then, a pang of fright hit him. He was an awkward dancer.

Hmmm. Solution. Admit this to Patti, and she'll give me a few pointers. Yeah, she'll like that! Phew!

Everything was going to be okay.

Then, he thought, *God, why am I so neurotic?*

Fifteen minutes later, Brickley reached the two bulldozer bouncers at the doors, but still no Shipley. This didn't make him feel any easier, and he wondered if he was about to be stood up.

Okay, she might have horrible taste in music, but I'm still

wild about her. And she saved my life!
He decided to mosey on in and grab two spots.

* * * *

They called themselves "The Karkarians," and they knew much. They were a by-product of millions of years of parallel evolution and of what they called simply "The Gene." Yes, they knew about genetics. They learned much from their human counterparts. Through all those epochs of time, humans had learned little about them. Humans couldn't handle the truth, and that was good. The Karkarians existed on the fringes of human consciousness, in folklore as sea monsters, Leviathan, the merpeople, the Kraken…and shapeshifters of the deep. They were a wild tale for children and old sailors, but they were best known as a very big surprise to certain people lost at sea.

The Karkarian had little trouble finding the place as the glow from the rear deck of the Titanic Café twisted its way into the ocean depths. The creature slowly raised its wide, missile-like head from the water and curiously watched the crowd of partiers spilling onto the deck. On the beach in front of the place were several fishermen. Occasionally, one of their lures would plunk into the water close by. The thing resisted the urge to strike at them, but those fake fish were tempting!

It did have a sense of humor. It grabbed the leader of the next lure it could reach, giving it a few tugs. Sure enough, an idiot human on the beach shouted, "Got one! It's huge!"

The creature toyed with the lure before finally letting it go.

"No!" cried the fisherman. "It…it got away!"

The Karkarian decided to wait a bit longer. It wished it could be sure that the "Chief of Security" was in that building.

* * * *

A wall of crashing rock music hit Brickley as he entered the dark, packed nightclub. The first person he recognized was the cafe's owner, Will Speeldebere, whose son had been in Brickley's 4th grade class that year. He was already tipsy.

"Bobby Baby! Happy summer! You here on business or pleasure?" Speeldebere boomed, grabbing Brickley's hand and shaking it vigorously. His breath smelled of hard liquor.

He was, after all, an alcoholic who owned a nightclub.

"Heard you had a little trouble at the beach!" Speeldebere called, but Brickley was already walking away.

The Titanic was a rough place. It had a reputation. The guys here were your classic biker-gang studs—huge, bulky, clad in black leather, with long hair and beards. At least once every summer, a fight between two young "ladies" over some low-life guy would turn into an all-out brawl.

Tonight marked Brickley's second visit to the place. His first, and he'd hoped last, had been the previous summer, when he was dragged here by some visiting cousins. They'd all been "lucky" enough to witness the annual brawl. Still, Brickley got to see Al Fergosi in action for the first time that night. Until then, Brickley assumed Sergeant Moron to be a farce...all bark but no bite. When most of the Easterly police officers on duty that night arrived, Fergosi took charge. He casually took in the scene, waiting for an opening, much like a surfer timing the breakers. Then, he and his officers threw themselves into the brawl, and within thirty seconds had each of the hulking bikers on the floor with hands cuffed.

Fergosi looked almost disappointed that it was over so quickly.

Hopefully, tonight will be a little quieter, Brickley thought.

Peering over a sea of bodies, the stage appeared hazy through Brickley's tearing eyes. The microphones were set, and the instruments were in their stands, waiting to be attacked. He looked at his watch. The band should start up in fifteen minutes, God help him.

Brickley plowed his way toward the bar to order a margarita. Yes, he was on call that night, but he'd be called only as a last resort, and he couldn't imagine for what. Answering phones at the substation, probably, while the rest were out doing real police work.

One drink won't hurt.

Brickley generally wasn't a drinker. A glass of Beaujolais while listening to Mozart in the evening, or the occasional bottle of beer. After all he'd been through that day, something a little stronger was in order, and he was still sore as hell from his Patti pounding.

A little alcohol might loosen me up for when she gets here.

Above the horde around the bar, Brickley noticed a large painting of a sinking ocean liner: RMS Titanic, appropriately enough. He also saw that it was going to be a struggle to reach the bartender. He decided to find a table and get waited on instead. He found one in a corner, where one petite, teen-aged looking girl perched. There were three free chairs. Brickley couldn't believe his luck.

"Anybody sitting here?" Brickley shouted against the cacophony of the crowd.

The girl's eyes widened, and a smile flickered across her face. She held her gaze on him for several seconds while her tongue-tied mouth opened to respond.

"No," she finally blurted, though Brickley couldn't hear her voice over the din.

He tumbled into the seat. She looked him over with a perky gaze.

"I'm Joya," she ventured.

"What?" called Brickley.

"My name is Joya Wolf," she shouted. "What's yours?"

"Bob. Bob Brickley."

They watched each other for a few moments until an enormous waitress suddenly loomed above them.

"Get'cha' som'n?" Her voice cut through the din like a train whistle.

"I'd like a margarita."

Then, Brickley thought, *when Patti gets here, she'd be pleased to find a drink waiting for her.*

"Make that two."

Wolf's face lit up.

The waitress disappeared into the multitude.

"So, what brings you to the beach?" Even though Wolf shouted her question, Brickley relied on his lip-reading skills to figure out what she was saying.

Why is the stupid music so loud? The band will be loud enough!

"I grew up around here. I teach at Tuckernut Elementary, but in the summer, I'm the village's security officer," he hollered.

Wolf was impressed.

Brickley hoped Patti would be able to find him. In fact, he hoped that she'd show up.

"I'll bet that's a hard job," Wolf piped.

"What is?"

"Being a security guy."

"Oh, uh, it's usually not too bad."

I'm also the closest thing to a witness in a triple murder, and the cops don't even know it, yet.

The waitress lumbered back with two overflowing, sudsy, lime-green margaritas. She set one in front of Brickley and the other in front of Wolf.

"Thanks!" Wolf beamed.

"Uh..." began Brickley.

"Fifteen bucks," the waitress barked.

Brickley gave her a twenty.

"Thanks," she said, and disappeared behind the wall of sorry humanity before Brickley could ask for his change.

Wolf sipped Shipley's Margarita. "Yum! Margaritas are my favorite!"

Oh, shit.

Suddenly, the earsplitting music stopped, and the crowd cheered. Brickley and Wolf looked up to see the Reckless Defecators take the stage. Actually, all they could see was the tops of the alleged musicians' heads above this heaving crowd of overgrown kids. One had green hair, two had no hair at all, and the fourth was clean-cut, looking very out of place. Explosions from the drums and guitars mugged Brickley's eardrums as the tribesmen tuned their instruments.

What am I going to do when Patti shows up?

Brickley became even more jumpy, drained his drink, and ordered another.

"All right," bellowed one of the Defecators. "Are you ready to party?"

An already very drunk biker momma screamed back, "What da ya think we been doin', you stupid fu..." Her last word was drowned out by a roar from the crowd. There was the crash of a dissonant guitar chord and the pounding of drums, which punched into Brickley's brain like a can opener. He drained his margarita and ordered another.

By this time, Brickley had drunk more than he ever had in his life, but the alcohol felt good, and he started to relax. He had a hunch that Shipley wasn't going to show, and that was fine with him. In fact, almost everything was becoming fine with Brickley. Being the big almost-eyewitness didn't even stress him, and he didn't feel claustrophobic anymore. Even though his eardrums ached, he actually found himself enjoying the music. The band was well-rehearsed, tight, and the notes of the lead guitarist's machine-gun licks were utterly clean. He turned his full attention to the music, only pausing to order another margarita. Boy, those drinks were going down smoothly! He looked around at the sloshy, tipsy room. This was fun! He glanced at Wolf, who was looking right at him. Her drink was still half-full.

Brickley stood to try and get a better view of the stage. The entire room swayed, and he grabbed the table to hold himself upright. Wolf stood as well, but then she noticed an arm extend from behind the wall of people and tap Brickley on the shoulder. He turned, shocked, and smiled a nervous, lopsided smile. He suddenly forgot that Wolf ever existed.

"I'm sorry I'm so late," shouted Patti Shipley. "A friend called me from Europe just as I was walking out the door. Are you mad?"

Brickley grinned like a mule. *Mad? I'm thrilled to death that you're even talking to me!*

"No way! I knew you'd come," he shouted over the blasting music to the woman who had saved his life.

Wolf glared at the intruder as Shipley cupped her hand to Brickley's ear.

"Let's go back to my place," she whispered loudly.

Brickley practically spit out the sip of margarita he'd just taken. He went blank, felt a surge of panic, then looked toward the stage, where the Reckless Defectors were wailing away on a screaming-fast song. He actually wanted to hear more music.

Reading this, Shipley shouted, "The Defectors come around a lot. Don't worry. We'll get to see them, again. I've got a bit of a headache, and this big crowd isn't helping. And I feel guilty 'cause I left little Fritzie alone too many times this week, and he's such a good dog. Did you know I just rescued a dog? He's so cute! He has a big vocabulary?"

"Vocabulary?"

"He understands when you talk to him! If you say, 'Fritz, wanna go for a walk?' He'll wag his tail and go get his leash! If you say, 'Fritz, wanna eat?' He'll wag his tail and bring you his bowl. He's so proud of himself, too! Oh, he's my little baby! Let's hang at my place! It's only a five-minute walk from here."

Wolf was steaming. She couldn't believe this! "Who's your friend?" she hollered, but they were so involved with each other, they didn't hear her. That made her even more steamed.

Brickley drained his margarita and managed to set the empty glass on the table. Wolf stared as this bitch grabbed Brickley by the arm and pull him into the sea of bodies.

The words "embarrassment" and "anger" didn't quite do it.

How dare that...that...whore take that guy away from me?

Wolf had been unlucky with guys, and she was lonely. She could tell right away that Brickley was different. She knew she'd never be able to forget a guy like him. Her uncomplicated mind started to work.

I'll find you, bitch, because Joya Wolf gets what she wants, and God help you if you get in my way!

* * * *

Brickley had to concentrate hard to keep up with Shipley, who dodged and ducked through the crowd with the agility of a running back. He used an old trick he'd learned as a defenseman so he wouldn't get faked out by the guy with the ball: Focus on their fulcrum, the area above the thighs and below the belt. A runner can easily fake moves with his head and shoulders, but not with his balance center. Thus, Brickley focused on Shipley's derriere. The margaritas weren't helping. At one point, Brickley ducked left with his elusive date, only to find himself staring at a blockade of human backs after she quickly darted to the right to exploit a better opening. The wall of people closed in around him, making his separation from Shipley complete, until her arm thrust out from nowhere to grab him and pull him through, again.

They were at Shipley's house in minutes. On the walk over, Brickley realized that his bladder was very full, and all he could think of was getting to her bathroom. He also had an urge to spit. The margaritas built up a tremendous wad of phlegm in his throat, but he didn't want to let loose a hawker of the volume it threatened to be in front of his spectacular date. Instead of spitting, he concentrated on not choking.

"My roommate's probably asleep by now. Be real quiet, so Fritz doesn't start yapping," Shipley told him.

Before entering the two-story house, Shipley realized she'd forgotten to get the mail from her box across the street.

"Oh, darn. I'll be right back. You head on in."

"Where's your bathroom?"

"Go down the hall, turn the corner, first door on the left."
"Thanks." Brickley opened the door.

* * * *

The lights of the Titanic Café loomed closer, and the sounds of 400 people partying to violent rock music filled the Karkarian's ears as it lay in the shallows, its right eye the only thing above the waves. Staring at all those people, it thought, *I could eat like a king!*

The creature was well within range of the fishermen on the shore. Several casts had already whistled over his head, and he had to slip to the side a few times to avoid getting nicked. It studied the cafe's layout. The back deck had four open doors. There was another door along the side that had a freestanding wall separating it from the parking lot, but the loud music and the flashing lights worried the creature.

This won't be easy.

It glided to a spot devoid of fishermen and stepped to the shore.

* * * *

Wobbling his way down the hall, Brickley found the bathroom, closed the door behind him, tried standing in front of the toilet, but found that it was swaying to and fro far below him. Fighting vertigo, he pulled his pants down and decided to sit, just to be on the safe side. He noticed a second door on the opposite wall. While his bladder let loose, he stared at the second door, which came in and out of focus. That was when he realized that the door was slightly ajar. Finished, but with his pants still down around his ankles, Brickley waddled across the floor to shut it.

Suddenly, a dog's nose appeared from behind it at doorknob height. It gently pushed the door open, and Brickley found himself staring face-to-face with the largest German shepherd he had ever seen. The animal, its eyes heavy with sleep, flinched back, startled at the sight of this stranger. All at once, the dog bolted fully awake, and its expression quickly turned from shock to outrage.

"Oh, shit!" gasped Brickley.

With an agility unknown since his football days, Brickley

sprang backward just as the dog lunged, his vise-like jaws crashing shut in empty air where Brickley's manhood had been a split second earlier. Brickley slammed himself into a far corner of the bathroom. His terror-stricken eyes locked with the dog's furious orbs, but all Brickley could see were those dripping canine fangs. This had to be cute little Fritz.

He dared Brickley to make a move.

"Good dog! Cute little pooch!" Brickley tried, but Fritz wasn't buying it. He growled steadily.

Ever so slowly, Brickley reached down to pull up his pants, but the growl rose as if to say, "Don't you dare!"

Suddenly, the German shepherd darted forward, and Brickley shot straight back up against the wall.

This is not good! What do I do? Gotta' think! Gotta' cover my jewels!

"C'mon, dog!" Brickley pleaded. His mind worked as furiously as his heart was pounding. "Good boy. Hey! Wanna' go for a walk?"

Fritz glared in utter contempt at the pantless scum cowering before him.

Even slower than before, Brickley's hands dipped gently downward, and Fritz's ominous rumbling kicked off again, changing to an all-out roar as Brickley's hands slid lower and lower. Fritz feigned another attack, and again Brickley snapped back to his frozen, hands-up position, farting loudly while doing so. Perplexed by the report, Fritz cocked his head.

"Where the hell are you, Patti? Oh, Patti! I know! Hey, boy. Wanna eat?"

Jeez, maybe I shouldn't say that one! This is ridiculous! I've gotta' pull up my pants!

"Freeze, mutha-fuckah!"

A short, crew-cut woman in a nightgown leaped through the doorway and aimed a 12-gauge shotgun directly at Brickley's face.

Jesus! Now what?

Brickley yelped as he snapped back against the wall, launching his hands into the air, leaving himself utterly vulnerable. His eyes leaped from the enormous weapon—it seemed twice the size of the person holding it—to the dog's fangs, bared less than two feet from his defenseless groin.

Fritz gave the gunwoman an annoyed look, as if to say, "Hey! This is my job!"

Brickley's mouth began flapping, but no words would come out.

"You got somethin' to say, rapist?" she shrieked.

"I...I...I'm no rapist!" Brickley squealed.

"Oh no! Of course not!" she said with mock sympathy, looking him up and down.

"You've just come to read the gas meter!"

Her gaze went downward. A grin spread wickedly across her face. She lowered the gun, pointing the double barrels at Brickley's limp member. Her hands began to shake, and the expression on her face got wilder and wilder. Laughter hissed from her mouth.

Back off, damn it! thought Fritz.

"Say good night, Dick!"

"I'm a friend of Patti's! I work as security for Tuckernut! I'm a 4th grade teacher, for God's sake!" he pleaded.

Then, Brickley heard the front door open.

"Patti! Help!"

The other bathroom door opened.

"Oh, my God!" cried Shipley. "Jane, he's a friend." Shipley's shock quickly melted into tenderness as she faced the dog. "It's okay, Fritzie! It's okay, boy," she cooed. "Good boy! Good boy, Fritz!" She pressed her ear against the dog's head and scratched his neck vigorously.

Good boy? thought Brickley incredulously as he still stood, hands up, backed into the corner, his penis dangling practically in their faces. Fritz's eyes remained locked on Brickley's.

The gunslinger pointed the weapon back at Brickley's face and asked, "It's okay?" sounding almost disappointed.

"It's okay, Jane. He's harmless," Shipley smiled.

"Harmless," echoed Brickley.

Jane lowered the weapon and said, "I'm glad I didn't shoot you," and left. She didn't sound too convincing.

Brickley groaned.

Patti looped an elegant finger through Fritz's collar and gently pulled him out of the room, but not before Fritz gave Brickley one more looking over.

"Sorry about this, Brickley," she said while fighting a losing battle to keep from grinning. "I'm really embarrassed."

"*You're* embarrassed?" He finally got to pull his pants up.

"My room's upstairs. C'mon up."

* * * *

Back at the Titanic Café, those closest to the back doors noticed it first. The raucous party that was in full swing on the back deck suddenly ceased. They realized that the entire crowd was silent and made a large space in the center of the deck. Their eyes were riveted to the dripping wet, seven-foot, barrel-chested man of 350 pounds of nothing but muscle standing stark naked in the center. He brought with him a miasma of danger that everyone's primal instincts registered. His piercing gaze met that of every cringing, cowering male on the deck. Certain that the "Chief of Security" wasn't among them, the massive figure turned to walk inside. The crowd parted instantly, revealing two very nervous bouncers who tried to remain tough-looking as this naked hulk stalked toward them.

"It's a fuckin' terminator!" someone from inside shouted.

"Uh, you...you can't come in here, p-pal," one of the bouncers stammered.

"What?" the apparition shouted in a wet, thundering rasp. He leered down at the six-foot, four-inch ex-football player and dripped seawater on his shoes. The bouncer felt a chill blast through his body as his eyes met eyes that looked far more like those of a shark than a human's. His mouth moved, but the words got stuck in his throat. The monster shoved past him and entered the Titanic.

* * * *

Brickley tightened his belt and started up the stairs to Shipley's bedroom. He felt for his smart phone and wished it would ring. His heart was still trying to handle the excess adrenaline, but his breathing was almost normal, again. His phlegm buildup had also been taken care of for now. Shipley peeked from around the banister.

"Brickley, I'm really sorry," she said, trying not to laugh.

"Well, now I have something to talk about at parties for years to come."

As he reached the top of the stairs, he stopped cold. "Where's Fritz?"

"In my room."

"*Your* room?"

"Yes. That's where his bed is. Don't worry. He knows you're my friend."

A Little Night Fishing

"Don't worry," Brickley said blankly.

Like an infantryman in hostile territory, Brickley crept warily behind Shipley as she led him down the hall. Her room was lit by two candles on a stand next to the bed. A futon rested on the floor. He spotted Fritz in the corner, lying on his doggie bed. Fritz's ears furled back, and his lips curled.

"Now Fritz, this is my friend Brickley. Brickley, this is Fritz."

"We've met."

Brickley heard that now-familiar, panzer-like rumble emanating from the German shepherd.

"Fritzie," Shipley fussed. "Brickley is a good friend of mine, and any friend of mine is a friend of yours."

"Friend of yours." Brickley smiled at Fritz.

Shipley patted Fritz lovingly on the head. Then, she snapped off the lamp and climbed onto the bed. The candlelight flickered and wavered, and Brickley wondered if this wasn't what it was like to be in a Vietnamese opium den during the last days of Saigon.

Shipley thumped the bed with her hand.

* * * *

Everyone stopped gyrating to the noise of the Defecators to stare with great unease at the giant—this very big, soaking wet, naked man. Even the band stopped playing. They all felt it: *Danger!* The intruder gazed into the eyes of every male, and no one hesitated to make room for him as he moved threateningly around the room.

Will Speeldebere quietly called the Easterly Police. He then went to the stage and told the band to keep playing. They reluctantly complied. The singer screeched, *"Dry heaves suck!"* and the band tore into another fast-paced melody of screams and shouts.

Then, Speeldebere made his big mistake. He told the special effects person to get at it. The already-dim lights went off, and a spotlight focused on the mirrored ball hanging from the ceiling at the center of the room. It made mad flashes and beams shoot everywhere. A strobe suddenly added itself to the visual melee.

Then, all hell broke loose.

* * * *

The flickering candlelight made the walls, ceiling and floor slosh around in rhythm with Brickley's pounding headache. The play of the candle shadows made him queasy. He wanted badly to spit another wad of margarita-induced phlegm, but that would mean walking past Fritz to get to the bathroom.

I drank too much! he thought as Shipley wrapped her arms around him and tugged him into bed.

"I've never done this before," she whispered to Brickley. He wasn't sure what she meant, and she read this in his expression. "Moved so quickly, I mean. Hey, this may be our first date, but I've known you since we were kids, Bob Brickley, and I know you're a nice person with a great sense of humor, and that's a pretty rare thing among guys."

She stroked his chest as she spoke. "Most guys need to be so cool and in control. It gets old."

She rested her hand over Brickley's heart. It was pounding at a fearful rate.

"Oh my," she cooed almost as lovingly as she had to Fritz. "Are you still upset from the little mishap downstairs?"

"Yes."

"I'm so sorry!" She kissed him on his cheek, then his lips. Her hand stroked his chest, and she kissed his cheek again, then slid her tongue down his neck, causing Brickley's eyes to practically pop from their sockets. Brickley stroked Shipley's back, then looked across the room to see Fritz staring at him ominously.

Shipley kissed him again and lay on her back, holding his hand against an ample breast.

"I get the impression *you've* never done this before."

His penis was like a frightened hermit crab hiding in its shell. His stomach felt so bad that a sweat broke out down his spine.

"No, I haven't," he managed to say.

"That's okay. I'm kinda flattered." Her voice was angelic.

With her eyes closed, she wrapped her fingers into his belt-loops and pulled him on top of her, face-to-face. When she opened her romance-filled eyes, the first thing she saw was a rope of drool dangling toward her. Shipley's mouth dropped open in horror as she realized what was about to happen.

It was at that moment that Brickley's smartphone blared.

* * * *

A Little Night Fishing

On the sidewalk below Shipley's bedroom window, the same elderly couple who had reported the diver in distress two days before walked their white toy poodle. The sudden sound of a ring tone drew their attention to the window. What followed were the near-simultaneous sounds of hard slapping, then cries from a powerfully sick male and a horrified female, upon which the male voice switched to agonized, panicked screaming as the roar of an enormous, enraged dog made it a threesome.

The couple and the poodle froze in shock at the commotion blasting from the upstairs window. Furniture crashed. Glass shattered, all to the vicious, guttural bellow of a monstrous dog. Within a minute, the front door flew open, and a wild man burst out, blood streaming from a right ear that didn't seem all that securely attached. He high-tailed it faster than the couple—or the poodle—had ever seen any human run before, with a huge German shepherd hurtling alongside. The dog was biting the poor guy's buttocks, then leaping up to nip his badly bleeding ear.

Suddenly, seized by a paralyzing stomach spasm, the wretched man dropped helplessly to all fours and loudly heaved. The dog fell upon him. Struggling to his feet, the victim reeled around the corner. The hulking canine smugly watched his victim flee into the night, then swaggered back toward home in absolute fulfillment, stopping only briefly to smell the little poodle's quaking asshole.

* * * *

At the Titanic Café, the naked giant's gaze shot upward to the twirling, mirrored dome on the ceiling that reflected the staccato flashes of strobes, beaming thousands of sparkling, twinkling lights that danced wildly around the ceiling, walls, and people. Suddenly, the apparition screamed. It was an agonized, guttural, unearthly howl. To the unbelieving eyes of the hundreds present, its entire body suddenly bulged and pulsated, expanding into something that looked like the obscenely human form of a great white shark. Its jaws yawned wide, dislocating themselves from their joints, while its eyes rolled backward, covered by a lower eyelid. The thing leaped mouth-first into the glittering ball, collided with a crash, and then fell to the floor along with a shower of broken glass—and screams and shouts from the stunned crowd.

"What a show!" some drunken idiot yelled.

The thing scrambled awkwardly to its feet. What now rose before the bewildered crowd was a twelve-foot shark with arm-like and leg-like appendages. Show or not, this was a little too much, and the stampede began.

The creature reared back, its jaws gaping wide, its jagged teeth dripping with its own blood, and sprung again at the remains of the tottering, shattered ball. With a frenzied thrashing of its head, it tore the globe from the ceiling and swallowed it, then lunged at the strobe light, knocking over panicked, fleeing patrons, and bowling through the bouncers who rashly tried to tackle it. The torn wires from the strobe spat sparks that quickly ignited a poster of a buxom blonde barmaid holding four beer steins in each hand. Chairs, tables, and people tumbled everywhere as smoke quickly filled the room.

* * * *

The police scanner was blaring, and the dispatcher was so excited that she didn't even use the usual codes.

"Major brawl at the Titanic Café in progress. Many injuries, need backup and ambulances!"

Flash Swynecock and Lance Grebe swung into the Titanic's hard-packed sand parking lot, swerving at the silhouette of a six-foot man sprinting ahead of the car. Sirens wailed from all directions. Flash had his video camera this time, and it was ready to roll. It focused on Brickley as he ran to the side door and disappeared behind the wall.

As soon as Brickley rounded the wall, the petite figure of Joya Wolf, screaming hysterically, tore past him in the other direction. Brickley's momentum sent him crashing into the sprinting, blood-spattered monster immediately behind her. The thing's momentum sent Brickley sprawling back out the door, with the thing essentially tripping over him.

Had the creature landed on top of him, it probably would have crushed Brickley to death. Instead, he landed on top of it.

Christ! It's him! It's the maniac!

This didn't look or feel like any costume...and the thing's breath! Well, it wasn't human, and if it caught him in those jaws...

A Little Night Fishing

Maybe, Brickley's brain couldn't take any more that day. Maybe, he just couldn't feel any more pain or fear. Maybe, it was the booze. Maybe, he was just too exhausted or frustrated to care. In any case, his football instincts took over, and he struggled like hell to hold his man—or whatever it was—down.

That's just what the camera recorded.

Chapter Seven

The next day, viewers of the noontime news broadcast on the Providence stations watched spellbound as the two struggling shapes lurched from the shadows into the poorly lit parking lot—the six-foot man falling on top of the seven-foot wacko in the bloodied shark costume. Taken off guard and looking like nothing so much as the proverbial "fish out of water", the wacko thrashed violently to escape Brickley's grip, but Brickley clung on despite his opponent's incredible strength.

Wolf stood ten feet away, screaming as she watched the struggle. A blow to Brickley's head from the thing's open palm stunned the former football great. His grip loosened, and the wacko sprang to his feet and bolted across the dunes toward the water. The camera followed it until it disappeared into the blackness, then zoomed in on the bleeding figure lying crumpled in the parking lot. The hysterical girl was now kneeling next to him, her hands clasped before her as though in frantic prayer, screaming over and over, "You saved my life! You saved my life!"

Swynecock's on-scene video interview of the young, bloodied summer security guard was dramatic. Brickley was still gasping for air, grimacing with pain and, above all, numb with fear and confusion. Rhode Island's new hero mechanically mouthed clichés like, "I was just doing my job."

Swynecock obliged by asking dumb questions.

"How do you feel?"

"Like hell."

Meanwhile, the petite, sobbing girl clutched Brickley's arm.

"That costume had some pretty big teeth! Did it 'bite' you?" Swynecock smirked.

That was the only time Brickley faltered. "Ah, I'm not sure. At least once, anyway." He gestured numbly to a shredded ear, caked with sand and blood, as emergency vehicles screeched into the parking lot. Behind them, fire suddenly burst from a broken window as the Titanic Café erupted in flames.

By that evening, the cable news networks had picked up the story and video, with pungent comments from commentators about the "Hollywood quality" of the wacko's high-tech suit, and amazement that there were no major injuries in the stampede and subsequent fire.

Back in his apartment that night, with the 11 o'clock local news blaring in the background, Brickley banged his forehead hard against the table. He peeked back to his television to see the paramedics wrapping his wounds, gently pulling Wolf off his shoulders, and pushing the camera away as firefighters scrambled in the background.

"Why did I say that about my ear?" he scolded himself miserably.

Couldn't resist, I guess.

He lifted his heavily bandaged, throbbing head long enough to glance at the front page of that day's *Providence Evening Bulletin*, complete with a photograph of his blood-covered self, clutched in the arms of the screaming girl. Above it, the headline screamed "Local hero!" Inside were more photos. There were shots of the burned-out interior of the Titanic Café, with broken glass, tables, and chairs strewn about. Other pictures showed bloodstains in the parking lot, near the side door where Brickley had, as the reporter wrote, "...tackled the giant, drug-crazed perpetrator who had effortlessly resisted all four of the nightclub's 'bouncers' and who is still at large."

Meanwhile, the newscaster babbled on. "In other news, it was a busy night for the Easterly Fire Department..."

Brickley had turned off the ringers on his telephones and quit answering the door. There was a small crowd on the sidewalk outside. He gingerly felt the wad of bandages over his ears, held together by well over forty stitches. The prognosis was good, the newspapers reported. He had a strong chance of keeping his ear.

Even Al Fergosi had dropped by the emergency room the previous night. In fact, he treated Brickley with genuine respect, certainly without the usual sarcasm. Get-well wishes poured in from across town and across the country as major newspapers and magazines picked up the dramatic photo of the blood-soaked security man sprawled in the sandy parking lot, grappling with the enormous, shadowed figure. An inset showing the girl clutching the hero as flames poured from the shattered window behind them. The caption screamed, "He saved my life!"

Numerous, shaken witnesses gave the police wild descriptions of the wacko. Most had thought at first that he was part of the show, but Will Speeldebere had denied that. Most also said that the intruder had teeth like a shark, inhuman eyes, was eight to twelve feet tall, and seemed to actually change his form when the strobe lights kicked in, turning from "human-like" to "shark-like".

All witnesses eventually admitted, some very reluctantly and only after tough questioning by Detective Rick Angell, to being either intoxicated at the time or to having taken hard drugs that day. The witnesses were officially dismissed as "unreliable." The film footage was deemed inconclusive because of the poor lighting. One or two smartphone videos from inside the nightclub came to light, but these showed only confused jostling and a large figure once again obscured by dim lighting.

Brickley thought of the doctors stitching up his damaged right ear, and of the police photographer documenting every gash close up, even having someone hold a micrometer to the wounds to help estimate the lengths and widths of the teeth marks to the thousandth of an inch. This caused a pang of stress to seize Brickley's still sore stomach.

What the hell was that about?

On top of that...

Oh, God. Do I have a headache!

He thought of the woman who had saved his life.

Does she hate me? Her room probably still smells like vomit. I'm sure one hot date!

His head fell into his hands.

I've got to apologize.

Brickley was just reaching to turn off the television when he heard the announcer bleat, "Miss Shipley's quick response saved the house from certain destruction..." He thought he didn't hear correctly until he realized that he was seeing the front of Shipley's house glistening in the morning sunshine. Spellbound, he watched the view zoom in on her bedroom window, where charred, tattered curtains hung amidst black scorch marks that streaked upward along the window frame. Then, he saw Shipley herself, standing with the Tuckernut fire chief.

"This is an excellent example of why fire extinguishers need to be on each floor of any house, with a fire response plan rehearsed and in place," the chief beamed. Shipley smiled the bewildered, glassy-eyed smile of a survivor.

"Ohh!" Brickley moaned thinly. "That candle. I must've knocked it over when the damn dog attacked! Oh, my God, I almost burned her house down! My first date with Patti Shipley!" He covered his mouth with his hands.

And now, I'm talking to myself!

Then, a little hope flickered inside him as he thought, *Apologize. Be honest and tell her how bad you feel. This will be a test of her mercy. If she hates you, better find out now than later that she's not for you! This could all be a good thing!*

Then came that snide voice from his left shoulder.

Yeah, right!

* * * *

Brickley was told that he could take some time off with pay. He didn't want to be in that apartment, especially not with the media and other gawkers on his doorstep. So, the next morning, Brickley squeamishly changed his ear bandage, pulled on his security uniform, and slumped behind his front door. He sighed, straightened up, turned the knob, and pulled. Cameras flashed and strangers surged forward, shouting questions or asking for his autograph. He politely threaded his way through them and got into the Tuckernut security vehicle, driving the short distance to the beach. Some scrambled into cars to give chase while others ran after the Jeep on foot.

As Brickley stood at the end of the boardwalk to Tuckernut Beach, heads turned, people pointed and began talking excitedly. Atop the lifeguard's chair, Brickley saw the back of Shipley's head, her blonde hair pulled into a thick, perky ponytail that hung over the backrest, and Brickley's heart leapt. Fighting the urge to run away, and realizing that several of his pursuers were gathering on the boardwalk behind him, he stepped onto the soft sand and approached the chair.

Is she going to tell anybody that my blood was because of her stupid dog—and that the thing was defending her from me? That I'm the one who caused her room to go up in flames?

He was totally at her mercy.

Brickley didn't notice the petite figure staring intently at him from the west jetty. Wolf's heart skipped a beat as she saw the man who had saved her life.

Why didn't I help him fight that guy? she thought. *I just stood there and screamed like an idiot while it pummeled that glorious man. I froze! I failed! On TV! I'm sorry! I'll make it up to him.*

First, he'd bought her a drink. Then, he'd rescued her from rape or worse. Out of nowhere, he'd appeared and did all this for her. She was more than in love with him. This was her soul mate, of that Wolf was sure! She didn't believe in coincidences. He was meant to find an empty seat at her table. He was meant to save her life.

We're meant to have a wonderful future together!

Meanwhile, picking up on the commotion, Patti Shipley turned to see the uniformed "hero" approaching. When their eyes met, Brickley immediately started to sweat. Then, Shipley smiled.

Wolf's tiny feet made prints in the sand the size of a child's as she stepped like a timid doe toward her soul mate. As she approached, she noticed the lifeguard climbing down from the chair. Where had she seen her before? Wolf assumed that they were going to talk business: the village security dude with a town lifeguard. Wolf stopped cold as she saw them standing face-to-face, their body language suggesting that the last thing on their agenda was business.

Then, Wolf remembered!

This is the low-life bitch who took my Bobby away from me last night! But he came back for me!

Her small hands drew into tight fists as she watched in helpless shock.

Brickley and Shipley both grinned. Brickley then grinned wider and shrugged with relief, playfully swiping his forehead. Next, the lifeguard slut slipped her fingers through his belt loops and drew him toward her. Finally, in front of a gathering crowd, they kissed. The crowd went wild, clapping, cheering, and hooting.

Wolf's knees buckled, and she crumpled to the sand, her eyes still locked with horror on the couple. The cheers only twisted the frigid knife that slammed into her heart. In Wolf's mind, the face of Patti Shipley displayed itself like a wanted poster, dead or alive.

God, she's now my mortal enemy!

Suddenly Wolf's eyes cleared as her simple mind told her that there was still hope. She just had to figure out what to do to turn the misguided hero back to his true soul mate. Wolf pressed her palms together like an angel at prayer.

I'm going to kill her. I'll find a way.

Her eyelids fluttered as a serpent-like smile spread across her face.

* * * *

Brickley was giddy with joy as he nuked his microwave supper that evening.

Patti Shipley! Patti Shipley! Patti Shipley!

Then, he began chanting, "Patti Shipley and Bob Brickley! Patti and Bob!"

His mind, his heart...everything inside Brickley raced faster and faster until he got dizzy and had to sit down.

I'm so fucking neurotic...

On the table sat his landline telephone, the ringer still switched off after the day-long barrage from the media and well-wishers, and not to mention a few prank calls. On his belt, his smartphone was off, too.

Suddenly, What if Patti wants to call me?

He switched both phones back on. Almost immediately, the smartphone rang. Brickley's heart leaped.

"Hello?" he asked hopefully.

"Brickley, this is Al. How ya' doin'?"

Brickley sobered instantly.

"Doin' all right. How are you, Al?" he replied to his new pal.

Fergosi ignored the question. "I'm at the station now, and I just want you to know that a couple of visitors came by who're very interested in you."

"More reporters?"

Fergosi laughed. "Nope. The 'Powers from Above'."

"Who?"

"The FBI." Fergosi usually would have added, "...you moron," but not this time.

"FBI?" Brickley felt a pang of unease. "What do *they* want?"

"They read your report on the nightclub incident, then took a copy with them. They asked a lot of questions about your ear."

"They asked a lot of questions about my ear?"

"Yes, the one you almost lost to that wacko."

"What the hell jurisdiction does the FBI have in this?" Brickley asked with shock.

"Well, they might know more than we do! Maybe, the guy's an interstate fugitive, bank robber, national nut job. Who the hell knows? Apparently, they called the state police and our chief and told them they were coming in on the case. You and I know that guy's probably a serial killer, for God's sake!" Fergosi replied. "And the FBI guys confiscated the photos of your injuries."

"What?" Brickley whined. "They took the photos of my ear?"

"No."

"No?"

There was a pause on Fergosi's end, then, "Brickley, what did I say?"

"That they took the pictures of my ear."

"What about that statement is unclear?"

Brickley felt a wave of panic. "Are they going to examine the photos?" His voice rose an octave or two.

"No. They're going to make them into posters to have you autograph them so they can give them to their grand kids. *Of course* they're going to examine them! Put them under microscopes! Analyze the digital images in their super computers! You see, Brickley, your ear might be the only physical evidence anybody has when it comes to this looney! They even said they were going to construct a model of the jaws that bit you."

Fergosi paused. "Hello? You still there, hero?"

Brickley was mentally kicking himself.

I should have known that. Holmes would be ashamed of me!

Chapter Eight

It was dark, and he was here against every instinct in his body because the wacko was still at large, but Bob Brickley had to know the truth. *Who was this guy? What was this guy?* Brickley figured that this was the most likely place for another encounter, but this time would be different. This time, Brickley was well armed.

He braced himself as a wall of black water slammed into the beach and surged toward him, sloshing around the legs of his wet-suit as he held his new eleven-foot surfcasting rod. Tropical Storm Avril was now only 200 miles to the south and was approaching hurricane force. Nobody knew just where in the Northeast the storm would make landfall, but wave heights were expected to increase throughout the night and into tomorrow. Another low-pressure system was coming in from the southwest, pumping its own swells into the area— swells that mixed and joined with the outriders of the unseasonably early tropical storm. Together, this caused the waves to break from different angles, depending on which weather system they came from. The waves from Avril broke straight onto the beach, while the waves from the other system hit the beach at an angle. The effect was a wild beach-break that churned up the water, resulting in excellent surf-casting conditions on West Beach, so long as the waves didn't get too large.

Some of them were too large already, Brickley suspected. Besides, this was stress time. The FBI would reconstruct Fritz's jaws, and Brickley would look like an idiot, a liar or both. Fergosi would go back to calling him a moron with every other breath. Patti Shipley would probably join him.

Brickley mused about how easy it would be to end it all by just diving into the pounding surf, then seeing how close he could swim to Bermuda. Then, there was the wacko, who would come and go from the water. With any luck, maybe he really was half-shark and would swallow him in one gulp!

The local hero couldn't see any way out of this one.

Brickley noticed that the fog was rolling in, just like on that other night with the three fishermen. Now, the ghostlike crests of breaking, five-foot rollers emerged from the mist to pummel the beach, punch the air, and spray his dripping face. Thanks to the wind, his ear bandage was already getting wet, and the salt water was making the wound sting. Still, Brickley's mixture of despair over his own situation, and the morbid expectancy at the possibility of meeting the maniac again, gave him a sort of weird detachment. Staring into the fog, his mind started to drift even as he held himself against the waves at the seething border where land became sea.

Brickley knew he was in too far, but he didn't care. It was as if he was doing something stupid just to prove to himself that he really was brave after all. Besides, the greatest joy in his solitary life was standing for an hour or more, gripping that pole, only to thrill at that sudden jolt, to see and hear the reel spinning, and to know that a great living, unseen force was at the other end. Then, his complicated mind cried:

Hey, Brickley! Fish or no fish, only a water hound or a fool would risk waves like these, and on such a foggy night!

Being armed wouldn't save him if these rollers got the upper hand. Strapped to his leg was his diver's knife, in a place where he could get to it quickly. In a waterproof pouch attached to his diving belt was his portable police radio. In another waterproof pouch at his diving belt was his father's 1960's-era Smith & Wesson snub-nosed police revolver, fully loaded. He even had a set of handcuffs with him,

With my luck, I'll shoot myself.

Brickley wasn't used to guns. He had qualified at the police range as a summer job requirement, even though he was unarmed on the summer job. He wasn't sure how he would perform if he ever had to use a gun on a person, wacko or not.

He was getting tired fighting these waves, and his feet were slipping in the ever-undulating sand. He backed up a little and found it easier to keep his feet. Nervously, he glanced back every now and then, expecting to see that otherworldly shadow looming out of the mist. If the guy did show up, Brickley told himself that he would calmly set his pole down, radio for backup, then take the gun from its pouch and aim it directly at the murderer.

Or should I point the gun at him and then call for backup... His insecurity grew.

A Little Night Fishing

For now, though, back to fishing. After his nightmare with the live eels on this very beach, Brickley swore he'd never use them, again. Tonight, he had his old faithful bait—chunks of menhaden. Dead menhaden. With waves this large, he needed to have a sinker weighing no less than seven ounces to keep his bait from washing back to shore.

Once, as he glanced behind himself, there was a break in the fog. Up on the sidewalk, under a streetlight, he caught sight of an elderly couple walking a toy poodle. They stopped and peered, just able to make out the fisherman.

The man's voice called, "Any luck?"

That was when it happened. The top half of Brickley's pole suddenly lurched toward the sea, and his reel sang as the twenty-pound test line suddenly shrieked from the spool.

"Yeah!" Brickley screamed with fierce delight. "Go baby, go!" His gaze fixed on the spinning reel.

The elderly couple strained to see, tickled for the fisherman and glad for the entertainment. Then, they lost him in the swirling fog.

A huge wave slammed onto the beach, sending up an explosion of spray and sand, and knocking Brickley backward. He happily fought the ferocious backwash to keep his balance. It reminded him of his football days: Taking a good hit but not falling. The wash slowly hissed back into the water, the ocean voraciously sucking it in. Brickley dug his heels into the sand again, leaned backward against the force, and had to replant his feet several times as the sand shifted under his boots.

The reel suddenly stopped.

Now!

Brickley couldn't see them, but behind the line of breakers was a series of massive swells pumped in from the tropical storm, and among these was a mountainous line of rollers from the new low-pressure system. Just behind the wall of fog, the first swell began building up to a ten-foot crest. At the precise moment it started to topple, an enormous swell from the other system crossed it. Instead of causing the wave to simply build up and break where all the other waves broke, the combined power caused the new wave to surge forward well beyond the breaking line.

Brickley tightened the drag, then yanked his pole back. "Yes!" He whooped as he felt the weight of the fish pulling hard. It was solidly hooked.

Then, Brickley heard a gurgling sound above and in front of him. He looked up to see a black, white-peaked wall towering toward him. He had just enough time to hold his breath. The wave smashed into him with a body blow, slammed him hard onto his back and buried him, grinding his head into the sand like a bully. It forced the oddly tepid, sandy seawater into his mouth, then washed him, tumbling head-over-heels, up the beach. In the tumult, his ear bandage was ripped off and, judging from the agony of stinging, so was the ear.

Oh, shit! Oh...shit!

As Brickley felt the power of the upward surge ebb, he seized the moment to heave himself to his feet and dig them into the sand. He had no chance. The rush of seawater pouring back into the Atlantic sucked him with it effortlessly. Brickley's chest was ready to explode, but he still managed to hold his breath as he rolled into the next breaker, which hurled him upward only to slam him back down on the hard sand. The impact knocked the wind out of him. His body spasmed violently as his lungs involuntarily gasped for air. The backwash pulled him well beyond the breaking line, to where the water was hopelessly over his head. Then, it ground him against the ocean bottom. His ear throbbed like all hell, and he gulped seawater. He didn't know which was worse.

Brickley toppled deeper and deeper into unconsciousness. His last thoughts were simply that he was going to die, and a weird, carbonated darkness forced itself into his awareness. It smothered all but one harsh impression: Two enormous hands had just grabbed him.

* * * *

The petite girl stood in front of the hulking punching bag. Wolf liked going to the gym at late hours. She noticed that several college-age boys, probably football players, were watching her, unable to hide their amusement at the sight of a girl who seemed not much heavier than the punching bag she was preparing to strike. Wolf caught their leering, patronizing grins, which simply added adrenaline to her quietly seething rage.

She pushed the bag away from her. As it swung back, she gave it a harder shove. The heavy canvas bag arched upward, then sailed back like a giant pendulum. The little Ninja planted her feet, crouched in a solid stance, and set her stare at a point just below the center of the approaching bag. With a shrill, banshee-like cry, she shot her foot forward and slammed it into the bag like an antitank round, causing it to lurch violently upward against its own momentum. She then turned toward the now-stunned group of athletes, smiled meekly, extended her delicate middle finger, and jabbed it at them with one lightning-fast flick.

What gave the boys the creeps was that her gesture was not obscene. Instead, her thrusting middle finger was like a stiletto piercing deeply into their guts. They actually *felt* it...

* * * *

The agony from retching and hacking seawater displaced the darkness that filled Brickley's brain and prickled its way into his consciousness. He felt weightless, as though held by angels' hands, just above the heaving surface. Then, he became very much aware that he was wet and cold, and he was still coughing up seawater. The black memory of being pulled into the ocean came back to him. His eyes fought their way open.

Brickley found himself apparently floating on his back, heaving up and down to the chopped rhythm of huge swells. His buoyant wet suit must have saved the day, he thought, and was glad he'd chosen to wear that instead of his chest-waders, tonight. His throbbing ear told him one thing.

Christ! I'm alive!

Then, his right hand brushed against something right next to him. He instinctively grabbed it and realized that he was holding onto a small buoy. Then, it hit him. He was clutching one the dozens of lobster-pot buoys that were between 100 and 200 yards offshore. In the middle of the night. In storm swells.

Oh, my God!

Panic surged over Brickley like a tsunami, and he screamed for help. This only brought up more seawater and bile. Another agonizing coughing and retching fit cut his screams short, and he felt his upper body suddenly *lifted* by powerful hands. Even amid his violent gagging, he remembered that final sensation before he'd blacked out.

Hands?

As Brickley regained control of his lungs and stomach, confused terror took over as those hands gently set him back down in the heaving water.

"You are the chief of security, correct?" a deep, watery voice spoke, making Brickley yelp with surprise.

Brickley shot an anxious gaze to his right and saw the enormous, vague shadow of what it was that was holding him. Brickley's fumbling mind suddenly grasped who, if not what, this was, and he realized that he was about to die. Amid his choking, he began to hyperventilate as he suppressed the desire to scream, again. Then, he felt the sea surge upward and heard the unmistakable, waterfall-like bubbling of a large whitecap tumbling from above.

"Hang on!" the must-be-real-after-all, worst-nightmare-confirmed shark-man rumbled. Then, it ducked under Brickley, grabbed his backside, and pushed him up as the wave lifted them both almost seven feet, the gurgling whitecap washing over Brickley's head in spite of the giant's efforts to keep him above it.

Brickley slid down the back of the wave, leaving his stomach high above. The monster's head burst back up from the sea, and green pinpoints of plankton-generated luminescence danced in the inky, effervescent water around him.

"It is urgent that we talk!" the giant shadow burbled.

"Urgent? Talk?" whined Brickley, his head finally clearing a little.

"Very urgent!"

There he—it—is! The killer! The land-shark—man-shark—what the hell ever! Jesus, I must be dreaming! Maybe, I did die, and this is hell!

In spite of his rising panic, Brickley commanded himself at least to try to keep his head.

No telling what this monster will do if I freak.

A detached calm tried to work its way into Brickley's consciousness, but random thoughts kept popping into his head.

There must be some rational explanation for this, Holmes. Alimentary, my dear Watson...

God knew where his handgun was, though his knife might still be there. Brickley felt the handcuffs still secured to his diving belt.

"You're under arrest," he pictured himself saying to this seagoing gargoyle. Then, he giddily pictured himself trying to manacle the shark-man's hands, reading him his Miranda rights while five-foot swells washed over them. He didn't have the authority to arrest people. Could he arrest sharks?

The wind was beginning to pick up, and the monster boomed, "I'm sorry I hit you the other night. Are you okay?"

Brickley blinked. "Uh...yeah."

"What?" it roared, two inches from Brickley's ear.

"Uh, yes!" shouted Brickley.

"I kinda lost it at that place with the bright lights. I had a bad feeling about going there, with all that stuff flashing and spinning around. I knew you would be there, so I risked it."

"You went there to see me?" Brickley hollered.

"You're the chief of security, are you not?"

"Well, I am the summer security guard for the village..."

"What?" it bellowed again.

Brickley repeated himself loudly. "Okay, then. You might say I am a security guard, too. You could say an 'enforcer' in your language, and I need to tell you something. We both have a big problem."

Your problem can't be as big as mine right now!

Brickley was giddy with confusion, pain, and disbelief. "Are you going to kill me?" he squeaked.

"What did I just say?" it thundered.

Oh, God! It's related to Fergosi!

"That we needed to talk?"

"That, and I just saved your stupid life! I could have swallowed you whole the other day when you got your stupid ass stuck in the current by the jetty, but I helped you!"

Brickley suddenly recalled the "rock" that he never knew was there and that seemed to move.

"That was you?"

"Yes!" The beast was trying to control its frustration.

"You could have killed me the other night, but instead, you attacked the eel I'd baited my line with, right?"

"Say that again?" it hollered.

Brickley shouted it, again.

The creature listened with amusement. "He actually bit into the hook and took off with it into the water?" The thing rumbled with ugly laughter. "What a whale's ass!"

Whale's ass?

Another huge swell scooped them upward, and the white-capped crest smacked Brickley in the face, forcing water up his nose. He spluttered.

"What happened to those missing fishermen? Did you kill them?" Brickley blurted. He couldn't help himself.

Suddenly, an iron hook of a fist clutched Brickley by his rubber collar and lifted him high out of the water. "No," it growled in a way that scared Brickley more than anything, yet. "And that wasn't me who attacked your eel."

Brickley blinked.

"That wasn't me who chowed down on the fishermen from this beach and that jetty," it continued.

"Chowed down?" Brickley gawked. "They were eaten?"

"Yes," it roared. "That's the problem!"

The rising cry of the wind, coupled with the roiling sea and the thunder of waves crashing onto the faraway beach became like a mass threat.

"Yes, they were all eaten," the monster continued. "It seems that a bunch of us have gotten out of hand."

A bunch of us?

"Look, security guard. I can't tell you much, but think of me as a liaison between my people and yours. I wouldn't trust you with more than you needed to know, anyway. We are the Karkarians. Our 'bottom line', as I believe your kind says these days, is that we don't want to attract any attention. For all of history, until now, we've managed, more or less, to stay out of humanity's way. Though, over time, some of us picked up a taste for your flesh. You do taste pretty good! And your damned blood there is driving me crazy! I thought you said you weren't hurt!"

Brickley's heart went cold, and he realized that his ear must be bleeding. Another swell lifted them, then washed over. He stammered a loud comment of his own in this impossible conversation.

"A dog got my ear...but...but we know all about sharks! They eat people all the time!"

"Yes, they do!" his captor roared. "But we're not ordinary sharks! The point is, we agreed a long time ago never to go ashore to eat humans. Except when it comes to killing things, you're a pretty stupid race, but we knew that you'd discover us sooner or later if we weren't careful near your shores. With your warships and, now, submarines, you could do us some pretty serious harm. If we stuck to shipwreck victims, humans like that, we knew we'd be in the clear."

Brickley was quickly deciding that he wasn't dead. He was just going crazy.

"So, we taste like chicken?"

"I never had the opportunity to eat chicken."

"How...how...how come you can talk?" Brickley blurted. "You speak English!"

"I also speak German. Let's just say that all humans who go into the deep ocean and meet us don't necessarily get eaten. There's so much you arrogant morons don't know!"

Morons!

"During your last sea war, many German, British, and American vessels went down in this ocean. Gave us a chance to improve our language skills."

"You're talking about World War II! That was like seventy years ago!" Brickley yelled.

"We have long life spans, and we're wired for languages because, and I hate to admit it, our two species are far more alike than you think. But your damned depth-charge attacks made me and many others half deaf!"

His tone became accusatory. "Do you know how loud a depth charge is when you're close by? Do you? *Do you?*"

The thing was enraged. Brickley just floated there. Its voice became hoarse. "Then, you humans started shooting off nukes underwater in the Pacific. You killed some of us there with those shots, and turned even more into vegetables—dumber than real sharks!"

Real sharks?

"They had to be put out of their misery. And there's still a lot of resentment toward you stupid land humans for that. In fact, a lot of us saw that as an act of war and wanted revenge. That group is being kept in line—for now."

"Sorry," Brickley squirmed in the iron grip.

"But I digress," it went on. "So, this one flaming crab-ass of ours decides, to hell with keeping a low profile. He wants to turn this coastline into one giant banquet table. Now, he's talked a few more into joining him, and a few others and I are trying to find him and stop him before you dumb-ass humans finally catch on and try to exterminate us!"

Brickley had no idea how to respond to all this. The monster went on.

"Here's the real big problem. There's a rumor that one troublemaker, let's call him 'Otto', has been inviting his friends to an upcoming, uh, 'feeding frenzy', as you'd call it."

Brickley's eyes widened. "Feeding frenzy?" he cried.

"What did I just say?"

"Feeding frenzy!"

"Yes," the creature burbled. "A goddamned feeding frenzy."

"Uh oh," Brickley peeped.

"'Uh oh' is right. So, a lot of you humans are on the menu."

He knows about menus? Where does he eat? Restaurants?

"But we don't know when this feast will take place or where. We assume it will be any day now and will take place along this shore. The first victims could be on a ship, at a beach party, or something else. We need your help."

Brickley was certain he hadn't heard right.

"My help?"

The creature was angry, again. "That's what I said! Why do you have to answer everything I say with a question? Are you Irish?"

Brickley blurted, "Irish?" before he could stop himself.

The thing gave him a shake and let out a growl of frustration, then started roaring, again, "Think about what the target could be, moron!" Then, it calmed a little. "We have some ideas, but we need answers from you. You know the territory, and you've seen the asshole with your own eyes. Most of you shitheads don't even believe your own eyes. In human form, he usually wears cutoff jeans."

Where the hell does he get jeans? Maybe I don't wanna know.

"If you think you see him, genius, shoot him over and over with all the ammo you've got. The bigger the gun, the better. And one last thing. Don't tell anybody anything I've told you, or I'll eat you myself!"

Brickley plucked up the guts to get a little irate in his own right, and all this shouting was tiring and painful. "How can I get help if I can't tell anybody?"

"Find a way!"

How do I get into shit that a crazy man couldn't make up?

The thing wasn't finished. "If word gets out, and your people start looking for us, we'll organize and take out as many of you as we can. We don't have to wait for you to come to us, as you already know. If we're desperate enough, we can hit you how, where, and when it will hurt most before you can do anything about it.

A Little Night Fishing

"Do you know how many little towns there are on the Atlantic Seaboard alone? We could swarm in, do our thing, get away, and you nitwits wouldn't be any the wiser until it was all over. You don't want to see us desperate!"

Brickley shivered. He nodded, realizing that the fate of thousands might lie in his hands. Thousands, maybe millions, of lives were in the hands of a 4th grade teacher, now a summer security guard making not much over minimum wage.

The creature saw that it had made its point. "Be right at that spot on that beach every day just after dark, starting in two days. I'll want to know what you've come up with, starting on Sunday at dusk."

"You know the days of the week?" Brickley squeaked.

"Shut up! Just be there!"

Brickley got the point. He took another gulp of air. "Okay. Come close enough so I can see you stick an eye out of the water. I'll raise both my arms if I have something, and only one if I don't."

"That will work. If you find out anything before dusk, get in the water and start banging a pair of good-sized rocks together until I respond."

"Suppose 'Otto' responds?"

"Relax. I'll keep him away."

Relax?

Brickley dared one more question. "What do I call you?"

He felt the creature thinking. "You couldn't pronounce my name. Just call me 'Bob'."

Oh, God!

The thing released its grip and disappeared. Brickley, wracked with exhaustion and pain, now treading water, realized with horror that "Bob" wasn't going to help him back to shore. He ducked under amid the towering swells and tried to shout.

Startlingly, the thing's head popped back up in the roiling darkness. "What?" it asked with annoyance.

"If you don't help me back to shore, you won't have your new contact, anymore." Brickley could barely muster the energy to shout. "And could you get my fishing pole back?"

"Don't push your luck, runt!"

Runt?

Then, "Bob" relented. Resigned, it grumbled, "Wait here."

Brickley treaded water and fought storm swells until he thought his arms would fall off and his lungs would burst. Before long, the monster appeared, again. It grabbed Brickley's hand and shoved the prodigal fishing pole into it. He was astounded to feel tugging, and he realized that the huge fish was still on the line.

"There. Happy?" the shark-man sneered.

"Thank you," Brickley called.

"Bob" picked Brickley up and shoved him toward shore amid the breakers. The shoreward swells lifted them both and hurried them forward. As they neared the beach, both picked up a sound above the waves and increasing wind. It was the unmistakable wail of approaching sirens.

"I'm outta here. Be on that beach at dusk tomorrow!" the shark-man rumbled, then vanished.

Two police cars and a rescue vehicle screeched to a halt in the parking lot above the beach. There to greet them was the elderly couple and their yapping poodle. They led the rescue team with surprising speed up the boardwalk and then through the deep sand. The EMTs' gear was clinking and clanking, their leather belts squeaking, their flashlights sweeping sharp beams through the remaining tatters of fog.

"Over there!" the old man shouted. He led them a little farther, until they came to a sudden halt. Before them, in his wet-suit, stood Bob Brickley. He was pale, shaking, dripping, smeared with sand, and his right ear was bleeding. He proudly held up a flapping, fifteen-pound striped bass.

"Is there a problem, folks?" he asked.

Chapter Nine

Joya Wolf was satisfied with herself.

My God, nothing settles the heart like a clear course of action!

No uncertainty about choices for this kid! This was the day she would kill that lifeguard, Patti Shipley, and her twisted spirit was as serene as it had ever been. Now in predator mode, Wolf stood at the edge of the boardwalk to Tuckernut Beach and looked toward the lifeguard stand. Sure enough, Patti Shipley was there, her blonde ponytail bobbing over the backrest.

Wolf's eyes narrowed. Her nostrils flared, and her senses became sharp. Her gaze turned toward the sea, and the sight brought the first pang of doubt. The waves were huge, and the wind was strong. Storm-generated rollers broke one after the other, well offshore, causing a constant roar that dominated the beach. A red flag flying above the lifeguard stand, right over Patti Shipley's head, signaled that there was no swimming allowed.

There were just a few hardy souls on the beach, watching the surf, including a few frustrated young people with surfboards. Most other people were at home or at their hotels, getting ready for the storm or watching the news. Word had gone around that an evacuation was possible, depending on the nearly unpredictable path of now-Hurricane Avril. Wolf knew that the lifeguard must be there to make sure that nobody went into the water. A strong and expert swimmer, Wolf had enough wits to realize that there was danger here. Then again, this situation could be perfect for her plan.

I can do this!

She would have to sneak into the water, but instead of swimming out beyond the breaking waves, she would go out halfway. Then, she would do it.

Duck under water for a while, then blast to the surface. I'll thrash and splash, grab a huge breath of air, then go back under. I'll keep doing it until that lifeguard slut comes after me. *When she gets there, I'll snap an underwater front-kick into her stomach. When she doubles over, she'll go under. I'll just hold her there by climbing all over her like the freakin' drowning victim I am. I shouldn't have to use the knife.*

Perfect!

Then, Wolf noticed something that almost sent her into a real panic. There was a second lifeguard standing near the water's edge.

What if the wrong one comes out to get me? Oh, no!

She thought as fast as she could, then smiled.

It'll just have to be good timing. Wait for the right moment. If it doesn't come up today, I'll just try again tomorrow. Timing is everything!

Wolf set her backpack down in an inconspicuous place, then spread out her blanket. She placed a paperback that she had no intention of reading on her towel, and strapped a small knife and sheath to her ankle. Then, she sat and waited. The target was still up on the chair, and the other was by the water.

Maybe, they'll switch places. Then, I go in the water. And then she goes in the water—for the last time ever!

There was something else that could affect this plan, though Wolf didn't see it just then. She didn't see it, because it was under water. Although it wasn't hungry, Otto was in the throes of one of its cravings—the craving for human meat. Having managed to get past the damned "enforcer", it was trying to monitor the position of the bathers not by sight, as the roiling sea was too kicked up to offer any visibility, but with the lateral line and electric sensors dotted along its snout. The lateral line, something all fish have, was highly sensitive to movement, and it could pick up the vibrations of any object in the water, even a piece of driftwood barely rocking in the waves of an almost flat sea. The electric sensors, common in sharks, picked up the slight magnetic field that surrounds all living creatures.

Trouble was, no bathers.

Must be the conditions. But there's always some shithead...

In theory, Otto would wait for a swimmer to separate from the group. It would wait for its prey to duck under a wave, and then do its thing. Before everyone cleared the water, it would quickly snatch another, and then another! Otto had done this twice during shipwrecks at sea but never near a beach.

Times they are a'changin'!

* * * *

Wolf's heart leaped when the guy lifeguard—a young, six-foot-plus Army veteran with bulging muscles who rejoiced in the name Henry "Hulk" Hoagland—turned away from the water and headed back toward the chair. Shipley jumped down, and they started talking.

Now!

Wolf started walking absently toward the pounding surf, showing no intention of entering the water. Almost there, she realized that the two lifeguards were still looking in the other direction. She started to run. Then, with a deer-like spring, she dove into a huge incoming breaker and started to pull for her life.

"Hey!" yelled a girl in the knot of people up the beach. "Somebody just dove in!"

Wolf didn't hear. She was starting to enjoy this. The water here was almost always frigid this early in the year, but was warmer than usual because of the approaching hurricane. The current was bad, though. She popped to the surface about thirty yards out amid huge swells. When she was at the crest of one, she caught sight of her intended prey running toward the water, blowing her whistle and pointing at her.

Ha! So far, so good!

Wolf immediately noticed that the current was pulling her rapidly to her left and away from the beach. For the first time, she started to wonder if this was such a great idea.

Well, it's now or never!

Not far away, Otto was thinking exactly the same thing as it sensed this one, lonely bather.

Even in the troughs of the waves, Wolf could hear the shrill blare of the whistle. When it stopped, she knew that Shipley had entered the water. At the near edge of the group on the beach, Flash Swynecock started cranking off photographs.

* * * *

The morsel Otto was tracking was suddenly thrashing around, which made it utterly irresistible. Then...wait! There was another one, a bigger one! Farther away but headed in this direction! Otto was in heaven!

Wolf repeatedly ducked under and burst to the surface again, and it wasn't entirely an act. She really was starting to panic. Shipley swam toward her with powerful strokes, up the crests and down the troughs of the six-foot swells.

Otto's lateral line told it that its appetizer was exactly thirty feet away. Sensing a helpless creature gave it such a high! Its heartbeat quickened, and at a distance of thirty feet, it could distinguish the sounds of human splashes from those of the waves, which made it giddy with excitement.

I'll have some fun with this little one first! Work up an appetite!

With a burst of speed, it darted forward, sliding under its target. With a mighty thrust of its tail against the sandy bottom sling-shotting it upward, Otto rammed into Joya Wolf's midsection, flinging her, shrieking, high into the air. The twelve-foot shark then breached the water in plain sight of the people on the beach. They stood in stunned awe, then all started screaming at once. His own mouth open, Swynecock kept on clicking.

The first thing Shipley heard was Wolf's hideous scream. Then came the yells from the beach. Instinct told her that something was very wrong.

Get back to the beach! Now!

Fighting every instinct in her body, Shipley surged against the enormous swells with herculean strokes as Hulk Hoagland ran to the water's edge with the rescue buoy. Wolf screamed with a guttural power that Shipley had never heard, before hitting the water again, only a few feet from where the dorsal and tail fins of the shark still churned the water.

Back on the beach, Flash Swynecock was in photographer's heaven.

* * * *

As Wolf plunged back under the surface, Otto was ready for the kill. Just as it was about to thrust forward, its lateral line registered the rapidly advancing swimmer, the bigger one. This one was too close to resist, but before Otto even had a chance to turn, a stinging pain suddenly shot through its body. Something had stabbed its left nostril. It hadn't felt pain like that in its life! In the monster's experience, distressed humans in the water seldom carried weapons. Its first reaction was to wrench away from this stabbing, fighting little human. Its second was to become blinded with rage. At the same time, Otto sensed the rapid approach of the other swimmer. It

A Little Night Fishing

would tear both of them to bloody pieces, and victim number two was now only ten feet away.

Otto wouldn't make the same mistake, again. It was kill now or nothing. Lunging forward, its powerful tail thrusting against the bottom, Otto launched itself upward, enormous jaws open. Thanks to the wound, the pain, and its own blood trailing into its eyes, Otto's aim was slightly off. Instead of biting down on this powerful human, its snout slammed into Shipley's stomach, tossing her eight feet through the air like a rag doll.

As she hit the water, the thing lunged at her, again. Screaming, Shipley clawed at the monster, and somehow, her thumb found its eye. She dug it in with all her strength. This pain was too much for Otto. With frightening power, it ripped itself away with a massive thrust of his tail. It sped to deeper water, its left eye bleeding and blinded, its nostril trailing blood and on fire with searing pain.

Instinctively ignoring his own stark terror at what he'd just seen, Hulk dove headlong into the sea and stroked harder than he ever had in his life. It matched any brave deed he'd ever done in combat. Shipley, dazed and battling for breath, was being pulled out by the riptide. Then, she sank beneath the crunching force of a six-foot Atlantic breaker.

Just then, Joya Wolf came bursting back to the surface. She gulped air and fought to get her panic under control. She looked around frantically, trying to get her bearings in the roiling sea and rising wind. It was then that she spotted the body of Patti Shipley bobbing face down about ten feet away. Instinctively, Wolf thrust forward, grabbed Shipley's body, and rolled her over. With Wolf holding her head, the lifeguard heaved violently as she spat up seawater.

Another breaker reared skyward. Wolf heard it before she saw it. Covering Shipley's face with her hand, Wolf took her under. Seconds later, they surfaced awkwardly in the churning white brine of the broken wave. To her own amazement, Wolf suddenly felt the hard, sandy bottom. She lifted the barely conscious Shipley's head above the rolling waves.

My God! This was meant to happen! I should be dead! Wolf's brain screamed.

It was just then that Hulk arrived with the flotation buoy.

"I'm okay!" Wolf shouted against the turmoil of wind and wave. "She's not!"

Hulk thrust the buoy against Shipley's body and wrapped its handles around her arms. Wolf helped keep Shipley's head high. She and Hulk turned to see another breaker about to topple over them. It scooped the three struggling swimmers into its tube, then spat them out from its crest, sending them on a five-foot, cart-wheeling free-fall. The wave crashed on top of them, actually pushing them closer to the beach.

Several of the gutsier bystanders were running into the water to help. The two rescuers pulled Shipley toward shore, on her back and not moving. By the time they reached the shallows, a large crowd had formed, with Flash roughly shoving children out of the way as he fought his way to the front. The rescuers laid Shipley on the wet sand just above the wash line. Otto's vicious teeth raked her side, and several jagged wounds sent rivulets of blood streaming into the sand, turning it red. Wolf stood in the upwash of the waves, ankle-deep, staring down at Shipley as Hulk started resuscitating her.

Exhausted, desperately relieved, but also in acute pain from a huge bruise on her midsection, Wolf watched the water around her feet stream red with the blood of her intended victim.

I was going to kill her, but we were both saved from that monster by a miracle!

Wolf's head swam, and her knees began to buckle as she realized she was about to faint. Suddenly, everything was moving in slow motion. Shipley coughing, Hulk pushing against her stomach, numerous kind hands reaching to steady and encourage her, and then the beach lurching upward. As her face thudded heavily into the sand, instead of seeing darkness, Joya Wolf saw light.

* * * *

Within a day, Flash Swynecock's photographs were blazing from the front pages of all the state's leading newspapers, and several other newspapers ranging from Hawaii to Japan were carrying the dramatic images. One woman thrust above the water in the middle of an agonizing scream. Barely visible in the water below was what looked like the lower jaw of a monstrous great white shark, its teeth barely distinguishable in the froth. Another photo showed Patti Shipley, her back to the camera as she swam toward the scene, a shark fin clearly visible only feet away from her. In the background, a perfectly formed storm wave curled, white water just beginning to tumble from its crest. Another picture showed Joya Wolf holding Patti Shipley as the other lifeguard arrived.

Swynecock's photos were even published in color by *USA Today*. They showed the two women lying crumpled on the beach, gashes from the shark's teeth brightly visible on one of them. Additional photos showed the two survivors side-by-side in a hospital room, recovering from the ordeal, one having received over a hundred stitches.

The photograph's headline read, "She saved my life"—spoken by Patti Shipley of Joya Wolf. Credit was also given to the other lifeguard, a certain Henry "Hulk" Hoagland, for saving the lives of the two women. Still other photographs showed Wolf, Shipley, and Hoagland at the hospital, receiving civilian medals of valor for their brave deeds. It wasn't everyone who wouldn't hesitate to strike out into rough seas to help a person who was being attacked by an enormous shark.

Nobody asked why Joya Wolf was in the water in the first place, but what the hell? Flash Swynecock had become famous!

Meanwhile, at an FBI crime lab, the re-creation of the jaw of the Titanic Café attacker was nearing completion. From the looks of it, agents might have to pay Mister Robert Brickley a visit.

Chapter Ten

The morning after the shark attacks, a police car squealed around the sharp curve and screeched to a halt in the Breachway parking lot. The door flew open. An enormous police sergeant squeezed out and, squinting seaward in the stiff, onshore wind, lifted a pair of binoculars to his eyes. Seconds later, the Tuckernut security Jeep pulled up behind the cruiser and parked carefully between the lines of a parking space. Emerging from the vehicle, with noticeably less alacrity, was the summer security guard, bandaged head and all. The sergeant said something to him without taking his binoculars off whatever he was peering at, after which the security guy raised a pair of binoculars to his own eyes.

Because of the approaching storm, the National Weather Service had issued a small craft advisory and a high wind warning, and there wasn't a pleasure boat to be seen—except one. Through his binoculars, Sergeant Al Fergosi could see the sleek, black *Shot Baker* darting among the huge waves— a floating gas tank kicking up tremendous walls of spray. On the horizon, the white-hulled Block Island Ferry swayed and yawed its way through the heaving seas on one of its thrice-daily journeys.

It was Sunday, and many people strolled the sidewalks to watch the surf and speculate about where Hurricane Avril would make landfall. Several stopped to watch the sergeant and the security man, and it wasn't long before they were joined by two boys on skateboards. Soon, there were ten people behind the uniformed men, with more coming up the sidewalk.

Wasn't that the security guard who was such a hero the other night? Are they watching sharks?

This time, however, Al Fergosi and Bob Brickley weren't playing games with the tourists.

"That boat shouldn't be out there in this weather," Brickley commented.

"She can take it. Look at that beautiful bastard handle those waves!" Fergosi replied.

The security guard didn't respond. His mind was far from slick boats, and he gave Fergosi a hard, searching stare.

What else do I have to lose? he thought.

Oddly, Brickley had an unmistakable feeling that he could trust Fergosi. That down deep, this big bully was becoming a good and loyal friend.

"We have to talk," Brickley said.

"What?"

"I need to tell you something. In private," Brickley persisted.

Fergosi looked at Brickley and could see that it was important. He'd noticed that the security guard had been preoccupied with his own thoughts all morning.

"Before you tell me anything, tell me a joke that will piss off my girlfriend."

Brickley stood there, confused.

"You know what a joke is, don't you, Brickley? I feel like pissing off my girlfriend when I get home. So, tell me an antifeminist joke, if you have one."

"I didn't know you had a girlfriend."

I like you, Al, but what kind of woman would put up with you?

"Yeah," Fergosi responded. Then, as if he'd read Brickley's mind, "I found someone who can tolerate somebody like me. I'm tired of her men-bashing jokes, and I really don't have any good comebacks. She's winning, Brickley. Like 'What do you call a man with 99 percent of his brain missing? Castrated.' And 'Why are all dumb blonde jokes one-liners? So men can remember them.' Oh, and 'What can a rooster do that a man can't? Eat with his pecker.' Ha ha."

"Uhh, okay. Why are divorces so expensive?" Brickley tried.

"Why?"

"Because they're worth it."

"Hmmm. Got a better one, Brickley?"

"If your dog is barking at the back door and your wife is yelling at the front door, who do you let in?"

"The dog, I assume."

"Why?"

Fergosi didn't know.

"Because once the dog's inside, he stops barking."

Fergosi slowly broke into a grin and chuckled. "Yeah,

that'll do the trick!" He chuckled some more. "Definitely. Thanks, buddy!"

"Al, I need to talk to you. It's important," Brickley persisted.

"Okay, shoot," said Fergosi. He was all smiles.

"Not here. Let's go where we won't be bothered or attract attention."

Fergosi gave him a searching look.

"Okay. I know just the place. Follow me."

Five minutes later, the cruiser and the Jeep rolled to a stop in front of a stretch of salt bog. Both drivers got out, and Brickley joined Fergosi, who was leaning against his car and raising his binoculars to his eyes once again.

"A common eider," reported the cop.

"What?"

"A common eider. One of my favorite ducks. Take a look."

Brickley saw the black and white bird through Fergosi's binoculars. So, the tough-guy cop was also a bird-watcher!

What else about Al Fergosi will surprise me? That he's related to a shark cop?

Brickley noticed that the binoculars were top-shelf, heavily built, and with a range-finding reticule in one lens. He looked next to the eyepieces and read, "Dienstglas 10 X 50. E. LEITZ, WETZLAR."

"Like them?" Fergosi asked. "I bought them at a gun show. German naval binoculars, World War II. Excellent condition. That's German optics for you. Did you know that in the United States submarine force in World War II, they loved to take photos through their periscopes, and the preferred cameras were German?"

A mosquito whined past Brickley's ear.

"Yes, I knew that," Brickley said. "As a matter of fact, I have my own pair of Leitz binoculars from the war."

Fergosi was impressed. Brickley swatted at the mosquito and missed.

"Not many people know or care, but German U-boats were cruising all up and down this very shoreline. But we got a few of them," the cop said.

Brickley suddenly piped up. "Fact is we sank one right off this point in 130 feet of water, in sight of land the day before the war ended." He pointed toward the horizon. "The U-boat sank a coal ship first. It took twelve men and one pet monkey down with her. I've dived on that U-boat."

A Little Night Fishing

"Really? Fuckin' Brickley, you dog! That's a dangerous dive. What else don't I know about you?"

With this and everything else that happened lately, Fergosi was realizing that he'd thoroughly underestimated Bob Brickley.

The mosquito continued to reconnoiter its target.

"So, what is it you need to tell me?" Fergosi asked. Suddenly, his hand shot out and two-dimensionalized the flying hypodermic.

The "enforcer's" warning two nights before, that Brickley wasn't to tell anyone about him and his race, to "find a way", replayed itself vividly in his mind. Fergosi could see that Brickley was jumpy as a cat.

"Look, guy. If you don't want me to tell anybody, I won't. No matter how intense it is."

Brickley looked hard into Fergosi's eyes and realized that he believed him totally. Brickley suddenly cried out and slapped a mosquito that was plunging its needle into his neck.

"Let's go for a drive. Hop in," said Fergosi.

The police car slowly pulled out of the parking lot, and Brickley decided to just go for it, come what may. He poured out the whole story, about the killer shark-man, then about the "enforcer" shark-man that called itself "Bob". Then, he told Fergosi about the attacks that might be coming.

Brickley stared out the windshield and braced for the inevitable torrent of laughter and abuse.

Why the hell did I just tell Fergosi all that? Brickley second-guessed himself. But the laughter never came.

Instead, in complete silence, Fergosi pulled to the side of the road and shut off the engine. Brickley hazarded a glance, and he saw that the big, tough cop was staring straight ahead, white as a sheet. His hands were shaking as he gripped the steering wheel.

What the hell?

Fergosi's mouth opened, but nothing came out.

"I know it's nuts," Brickley started. "I don't expect you to believe..."

"I believe every word you just said," Fergosi whispered, still staring ahead. "Be...because I just put two and two together." He was paler than ever.

The cop turned and looked at Brickley. "Those FBI guys at the station this morning..."

"What about them?" Brickley was staring hard at Fergosi. This was the last reaction he'd expected.

"They…I overhead something they said. I was in the hallway around the corner, and they couldn't see me. They said something about 'Carakians,' 'Karkanians'…something like that."

"Karkarians," Brickley corrected, his heart frozen.

Fergosi turned and looked at Brickley. "That's it! I heard them say something about them coming out of the ocean and killing people. They were scared shitless. I just thought I hadn't heard right or maybe even they were talking some kind of code. But with those disappearances, all that shit at the Titanic, and now what you just said…"

Suddenly, the police radio crackled in the background. Both men jumped.

"Shit!" Fergosi cried, but it was a call for another car.

"So, you do believe me," Brickley stated.

"Yes, but that's not the whole reason. What I heard this morning and from you just now was just the gravy on the potatoes." Fergosi looked down at his lap. The radio sputtered again, but no voice came out. A gust of wind shook the car.

"My father was a merchant sailor in the '50s," Fergosi began, turning to stare back out the windshield. "His ship went down in a storm a few hundred miles out in the Atlantic. He survived, but he was never the same, again. He left the Merchant Marine, came home, and became a fireman. We just figured it was the shipwreck, but I was with him at the hospital when he died ten years ago. That was when he told me about the talking sharks that wanted to know what was going on in our world. He said they caught him when he went into the water and started asking him questions. They ate everybody else. The only reason he got away was because a Coast Guard cutter got there and scared the sharks away. My father was the only survivor, and he never said a word about it before that day he died, and only to me. I was the only one there. I was the only one who knew."

Fergosi looked at his lap. "I thought he was just delirious or something as he was dying." He turned back to Brickley. "What the Christ is this all about?"

"Some kind of parallel evolution or something, only in the ocean." Then, Brickley turned to him. "I want you to meet this 'Bob'. We have a deal to meet at West Beach every night at dusk, starting tonight."

Fergosi's eyes widened as he looked at Brickley. "He's gonna come up on the beach?"

"No, not him, anyway," Brickley was starting to tremble. "I'm supposed to just signal him from the beach. But we'll see."

"Christ Almighty!" Fergosi breathed.

The radio crackled, again. "Unit six-nine, check for reported 11-26 at Post Road and Willow River Road..."

That was for Fergosi. "Fuckin' abandoned bicycle!" he spat. "At the end of the fuckin' world as we know it." He started the cruiser, turned around, and started back toward the Breachway. "Not critical. I'll drop you back at the lot."

They drove on in silence. Then, Fergosi asked, "Okay, so why would this alleged good guy try to bite your ear off at the Titanic the other night?"

Brickley groaned and remained quiet. In front of them, a car with a big Student Driver sign on its roof plodded along. Fergosi tailgated it, and the driving instructor glanced back at them. Then, Fergosi looked sidelong at Brickley. "What else is bothering you, as if this shark shit isn't enough? Let me guess, the FBI?"

Brickley shut his eyes. "I was thinking about warning them, but I didn't think they'd believe it. From what you say, they already know, thank God."

The student driver signaled a left turn and slowed, at least a hundred yards before the stop sign. Fergosi followed the car as it finally turned. The student's rear view mirror filled with the stalking police car and its stone-faced, hulking driver. The instructor looked back once again.

Fergosi didn't push Brickley to say more. They drove on at the student driver's snail's pace. She put on her right turn signal hundreds of feet before the next intersection. After an eternity of decelerating, the student stopped, dutifully looked both ways several times, turned right, and accelerated ever so slowly.

Fergosi turned right and kept on her tail. The perplexed driving instructor turned to look at them again, and raised his hand questioningly. Fergosi ignored the instructor's agitated attempt at communication, and he chuckled ever so subtly as he tried to keep a stern expression on his face.

"And you're doing this why?" Brickley finally asked.

"I recognize the driving instructor. Frank Slade. Sounds

like a fuckin' gunslinger. He was one of my high school teachers. He was, and still is, a total asshole," Fergosi replied. "Besides, it takes my mind off all this crazy shark crap."

"How long ago was he one of your teachers?" asked Brickley.

"About fifteen years."

Brickley looked at his feet, then broke out in a smile. "I never had him in high school, but I've heard of him."

"There's something else about the guy," Fergosi added. "I can't put my finger on it, but my instincts always told me that he was no good, right down to the core, like someday we'll be reading about him."

"Uh..." Brickley stammered, changing the subject. "The wound to my ear...um..." He took a deep breath. "That wasn't the shark guy."

Fergosi nodded, trying to look casual.

More silence.

"A dog did that."

A few moments of silence. Then, Fergosi repeated, "A dog."

Brickley then let the cat out of the bag about how he got his ear mangled by Patti Shipley's enormous German shepherd.

Fergosi remained serious, then gave a half chuckle. "Brickley, I'd be rolling in the aisles about that if I wasn't so shaken up by this horror show we're living. How the hell do you get into this shit?"

"Damned if I know," Brickley muttered.

"This moron's doing about 20!" Fergosi suddenly barked with frustration, turning his attention back to the car in front of them. He hit the siren and the lights.

The student driver suddenly shot forward, bolted off the road, and burst across the sidewalk. Her front end suddenly vaulted into the air on contact with a low, poison ivy-covered stone wall, sling-shotting the two occupants' heads into their backrests.

"Shit!" Fergosi cried. "Brickley, see if they're okay. I'll call for the rescue. Goddammit, I'm going to waste half the afternoon writing this up!"

"Don't forget to check for that abandoned bicycle," Brickley joked half-heartedly.

They finally returned to the Breachway parking lot, where Brickley's security Jeep waited.

"I'll see you at West Beach, tonight," Fergosi said as Brickley got out of the cruiser.

A Little Night Fishing

Ten hours later, Alphonse Fergosi lay in bed, staring at the ceiling. It was years since he'd had a sleepless night, but after who or what he'd encountered that evening at West Beach, the cop wondered if he'd ever sleep, again.

Chapter Eleven

Nothing is darker than the bottom of the ocean at night. Several miles off Tuckernut Breachway, the undiscovered wreck of a German Type X mine-laying U-boat rested on its keel in 250 feet of water. The scene was as opaque as ink, and one dependent on eyesight alone would be utterly helpless. Sea creatures, with their lateral lines and sonar senses, are as at home in the dark as they are in the light. For hundreds of yards, they can sense all movement and all objects. In this case, they could even sense the ragged hole in the U-boat's hull, where it had struck a huge boulder as it hit the bottom in 1944.

The shark-like figures rested on the forward deck, large-bellied and with gaping mouths. A series of sharp grunts, clicks, and squeaks emanated angrily from one of them as it spoke to them in their own language. Its nostril was still red from the stab of Joya Wolf's knife, and its swollen, blinded eye oozed.

The members of Otto's cadre dutifully listened. Otto was the largest and most violent of the group, and its followers were terrified of it. Except, that is, for two of them. Both might have been wary of Otto, but neither was terrified of him.

One of these was Otto's mate. Like a human "motorcycle mamma", it tagged along for the thrill of being an outcast among outcasts, and for the status of being the leader's "woman". The other almost-fearless creature was nicknamed "The Professor". It had tremendous interest in what shipwreck victims said about themselves and their cultures. It would milk them for as much knowledge as it could before its desperate cravings overcame it and devoured the victims in roiling frenzies. "The Professor" was the only one with the nerve to question Otto.

"Then, the little puke digs my eye out!" Otto spat with rage. It was in pain—great pain. "I'm going to get that brat! I'm going to get them all!"

The others listened intently. Otto was more furious than they had ever seen it, and their guards were up.

"I think it's time for our little feast."

They clicked and grunted in agreement.

"In fact, I'd like to see to it that there are far too many humans in the water for us to eat. I mean, there'll be so many helpless humans, we'll wind up tearing most of them to shreds without eating them. We're going to bite off heads, arms, and legs just for the fun of it! We're going to have tugs-of-war, contests to see who can hold the most human heads in their mouths!"

Otto raged on, and their unease grew. The last time it had raged on anything like this, it had struck out and torn one of their comrades to bloody shreds. It was a horrifying scene, even for such dedicated bloodthirsty monsters. Still, the cloud of blood that filled the water was too much for the shocked witnesses. In spite of their horror, they too had attacked with vicious abandon what was left of their hapless comrade.

Otto stopped raving and started furiously opening and closing its maw to pump water through its twelve gills. This seemed to calm it a bit. Then, Otto turned its gaze almost lovingly toward the rusted metal containers on the forward deck of the U-boat. Visible through the thickly rusted gashes riddling the containers were metallic spheres. Unexploded mines.

"We've got at least six mines here that will still work," Otto beamed proudly. It then slapped the sides of the lethal containers several times, sending rusted chunks of metal flying and causing the others to cringe and cover their heads. It ignored them.

"We'll take them to the shipping lanes between Block Island and the mainland. We'll anchor three in the path of that white ship that shuttles back and forth so many times during the day. It's loaded, and I mean *loaded*, with humans. We'll put the rest of the mines in a pattern around those three."

Otto pumped more water through its gills, then looked at its coconspirators and made what passed among these creatures for a smile. "Any questions?"

"Sounds good, boss!" one clicked.

"I like it!" another squeaked.

"I'm already hungry!" grunted a third.

Then came "The Professor". "Won't the explosions kill us? Those mines exploding will send a shock wave through the water that will burst every organ in our bodies, just like all those depth charges during the..."

"Yeah, they'll do that if you're stupid enough to hang around. After we anchor them, we watch from a good distance,". Then, Otto put his hideous face an inch from 'The Professor's'.

"You stupid, goddamn moron!"

The others ducked their heads or stared straight ahead, afraid to move.

Undaunted, "The Professor" continued. "I have another question." The others wished he'd shut up.

Otto glared at him.

"Won't the sound of the explosions attract the *electis* and his squad of do-gooders? We know they've been looking for us, especially after what just happened with you at the beach," "The Professor" continued, not noticing the pleading in his comrades' eyes. "If they haven't found out about that already, they're bound to. And they'll redouble their search."

"Are you afraid of them?" Otto" shot back.

"The Professor" hesitated. Indicating "no", he then fell silent, much to the relief of the others.

"Then, it's set," Otto pronounced. "And we must remember to thank our German friends for supplying us with such wonderful tools!" he announced, gesturing almost reverently toward the U-boat's deadly cargo. He raised his right pectoral fin in a shocking parody of the Nazi salute.

"Actually, the German Navy tended not to do the Hitler salute," piped up "The Professor". "It might be because they and Hitler didn't get along that well, primarily because of social class. Naval officers tended to be from upper-class families, and the Nazis made up largely of the so-called 'working class'. So, the Kriegsmarine gave the regular military salute instead of the Nazi—"

"The Professor" halted in mid-sentence because Otto's teeth tore out its voice box and spat it out. The wounded creature's intellect immediately grasped that the reason its voice box was darting in various directions was because it was under attack by a squad of ravenous minnows that appeared out of nowhere. Too late, "The Professor" became acutely aware of how urgently it had needed to keep its mouth shut and how unfair life was being. It next realized that it was losing all sensation from the pectoral fins down the length of its tail as Otto slammed its head against the U-boat's hull over and over and over...

"I'll fuckin' kill you! I'll fuckin' kill you!" it roared.

The Professor's blood joined the cloud of rust billowing from the points of contact with its head. The tail of the unfortunate intellectual suddenly jerked and thrashed in violent, involuntary spasms. This set the others off, and they tore into it with wild abandon. In less than twenty seconds, "The Professor" disappeared in a cloud of blood. Every chunk was soon in the stomachs of its former comrades. The smallest pieces caused a blitzkrieg of trigger fish, cunners, and minnows to churn the bloody water like a blender.

Then, everyone except Otto scattered as they realized all at once that any one of them could be next.

Within minutes, the current carried the blood cloud away. Slowly, one-by-one, its followers filtered back.

"We all agree to the plan?" Otto asked with mock solemnity.

All indicated "yes" without hesitation.

Then, they turned upward as a metallic buzzing faded in from miles away. The creatures could tell that it was a large cargo vessel heading for Narragansett Bay. Since the surface had become so rough, there was less marine traffic, and no small craft at all.

Then, Otto had an idea. "Follow me," he ordered. "We're going to have a little fun!"

* * * *

It was night at Tuckernut Breachway. Off duty now and in civilian clothes, Bob Brickley and Al Fergosi sat on the rocks on the west jetty's leeward side, sheltered from the wind and with a cooler of beer between them. In only the dimmest illumination from the lights of the nearby parking lot, they watched the storm waves wash up on the rocks. From the jetty's windward side, however, the roar was constant, the spray flew up and caught by the fierce wind, and the air was saturated with salt mist. They stared at the black water of the inlet, where a strong current swept islands of foam into the adjoining pond.

They were both surprised at how calm they were, given their "meeting" of the night before with a very irate "enforcer". This evening at dusk, however, Fergosi hid behind the rocks at West Beach as Brickley awaiting the daily "contact". But the "enforcer" hadn't shown.

They also found themselves wondering why they were here at the jetty, given the recent killings and what they now knew. They pleaded with the Easterly Police Chief to close the Breachway after dark because of the recent "disappearances", but he'd refused, wanting to know why they seemed so desperate about it.

"I haven't heard from the State Police or the FBI about any possible crime involving the Breachway area," she'd said.

Nevertheless, Brickley and Fergosi had arrived there this night to find "Closed to Fishing After Sunset" signs.

"Maybe those FBI guys pulled strings. A good thing," Brickley observed.

"Yeah," Fergosi replied. "I can't believe how that 'enforcer' freaked when he found out that you told me everything," he added.

"They have serious tempers," Brickley replied worriedly. "He said he'd eat me himself if I told. So, here I am, sitting by the water. Story of my life."

He tossed a rock into the swirling current, its splash barely audible over the roar of the waves. He found himself glad that Fergosi was with him.

"I don't know," Fergosi said. "I figured it'd be okay after you told him I'm a police sergeant. And he seemed really desperate. We're lucky we got out of there. Him not showing up tonight probably isn't a good sign. You packin'?" Fergosi asked suddenly.

"Is the Pope from Argentina?" Brickley replied.

Fergosi grinned, then popped open a beer and drained half of it. "Me, too. Any of those bastards show up, we're ready."

Brickley cringed. *Gawd! Just the sight of booze makes me sick!*

Besides, drinking in a public park like this was a misdemeanor.

"Al…uh…"

"Yeah, yeah, I know. I'm drinking on town property. Listen, Brickley, if people are being cool about it, not bothering anybody, not being obvious, do I bust them?"

"Uh…"

"No, I don't. Then, you get these jerks I busted the other day on the other side over there," Fergosi gestured to the now-invisible east jetty with his beer. "They attracted attention.

They were obnoxious. If I was a father, I wouldn't want my kid down here fishing at night with drunk jerks around. What do I hear but breaking glass, loud cursing, and laughing. So, I walk over, and there's one whiskey bottle lyin' on the rocks and another broken bottle with glass shards all over the sand that barefoot people like to walk on, and the smell of hard liquor was strong enough to knock you over. So, yeah. I arrested 'em. They weren't exactly cooperative, which is another reason I arrested 'em."

"Hmmm," hummed Brickley, taking a swig of water. "It's not just that. What if one of them—and I don't mean kids—comes along? We need to be alert."

Neither man heard the car glide to a stop in the parking lot fifty yards away. Even though a small sand dune concealed the lot from view, the driver had his lights off well before turning in. He disengaged the dome light as well. So, when the car door opened, only a shadow emerged.

"Beach parties," said Fergosi.

"What?"

"Beach parties. Think of it, a bunch of people gathered around a fire on the beach. How fast could the land-sharks take them? Very quickly, from the looks of that 'Bob' character."

"Yeah," Brickley answered thoughtfully. "Yeah," he said, again.

"Or boats," Fergosi went on. "Think of it. A mile or two out, and who's going to stop a bunch of land-sharks from boarding your vessel?"

"Uh huh," Brickley answered. "But with seas like we've got, there'll be no boats out there except for the big stuff."

"Hmmm," responded Fergosi. Then, he shook his head. "We've got a problem."

"Ya think?"

Fergosi looked at Brickley in the dim light, the constant roar of the sea in the background. "We have to talk to those FBI guys. We have to be sure they know what we know."

"I thought they'd wanna talk to me by now, but I haven't heard shit," Brickley stated. "And the coast is so big! I mean, how the hell are we—or they—supposed to predict where this...'feeding frenzy' is going to be? I mean, if it's a beach party, which beach? It's not too early in the summer for there to be bonfires all up and down the coast!"

* * * *

His gait was more like a gorilla's than a human's as he carefully picked his way to the sand dune separating the parking lot from Tuckernut Beach and the west jetty. Frank Slade, now wearing a neck brace, remembered how he'd gotten his foot caught beneath the brakes on his side of the car because he'd turned around so quickly to look at that moron Fergosi riding his ass and making the student lose control. Then, the asshole had wised off to him as the rescue vehicle arrived to check him and the student for injuries. The final straw for this overstressed driving instructor was when the two other cops arrived, then backed up Fergosi when he said he wasn't responsible for freaking out the student. The idiot security guard hadn't seen a thing.

Slade had spent most of his life mad at the world, and he'd finally snapped. He placed the steel ball-bearing into the pocket of the souped-up hunting slingshot.

* * * *

Fergosi drained another beer. Brickley took a swig of cola.

"I'm off tomorrow," Fergosi said. "That'll give me a chance to contact the FBI. I don't want anybody else at the station to know about this, okay? They'll think we're nuts. We could both lose our jobs."

"You're right," Brickley agreed.

The violent, snapping sound that surgical tubing makes when extreme tension on it is suddenly released went unheard over the roar of the sea. The steel ball screamed through the thick salt air toward the two figures sitting on the jetty. It grazed the back of Al Fergosi's head, and then altered its deadly course to glance off Bob Brickley's forehead.

* * * *

Their tails undulated in slow, steady unison, pacing themselves like long-distance runners. The buzz of a tugboat pierced the silence of the black ocean bottom as they entered the mouth of Narragansett Bay. It was early night, and they knew that the hunting would be better up the bay. There was a heavy chop, but it was nothing like the open ocean. There would be at least some small boats out, especially in some of the more sheltered inlets, and there might even be a night swimmer or two. As they swam on, bluefish, sea bass, and cod skittered away in terror. Though, they paid no attention. Soon, they heard tinny whines from the propellers of several smaller craft. Farther they swam, under the great bridge, past the lighthouse, and into relatively calmer waters. At a command from Otto, the group turned left and eased into Potter Cove.

Almost at once, a propeller buzzed twenty feet overhead, only to stop. They heard a splash, then sensed an anchor plunging downward to hit the sandy bottom with a heavy crunch as it pancaked a horseshoe crab that was in the wrong place at the wrong time.

"Let's wait here and see what this guy's up to," Otto told the others.

Within minutes, they heard the plunks of baited lines as they hit the water.

"Yeah!" clicked Otto. "Live eels!" It paused, consciously summoning its anger. "Do you know how those humans use live eels?

Don't they eat them? thought several.

"They hook them through their eye sockets," the leader communicated.

Its sonar looked into the faces of its pack, which stared blankly back. They didn't get it. Its anger was building.

"That's not okay, dig? That's ruthless. That's cruel. That's our job! Who the hell do they think they are?"

They weren't sure whether to laugh.

One echoed, "Yeah! Who do they think they are?"

"What scum!" another clicked.

Then, a third squeaked, "How would they like it if someone did that to them?"

To which Otto shouted, "Exactly! Now, here's what we're going to do..."

* * * *

The brand-new, eighteen-foot cuddy cabin cruiser swayed in the swell of the bay, anchored about 150 yards off the cove shore. It was just north of the majestic suspension bridge that spanned Narragansett Bay's East Passage, connecting Newport with Jamestown Island. Illuminated by a dim lantern, a large bucket on the deck writhed with a dozen doomed eels. Three men stood, holding their rods and feeling the slight tugs of the struggling eels on the ends of their lines. Except for wind gusts and the purr of traffic on the bridge, all was quiet.

Suddenly, a pair of enormous arms shot out of the water. Otto grabbed the gunwale and boomed cheerfully, "Any luck?"

Two of the fishermen jumped backward and yapped in surprise, nearly toppling over the other side. Then, several more huge, dark figures burst from the water and grabbed the gunwales.

"Jesus Christ!" one of the fishermen choked out the words.

Now metamorphosed into its almost-human form, Otto pulled itself aboard as the stunned men watched.

"Bay Patrol!" it announced. It looked into the bucket of eels and burbled, "You're not using *live* eels as bait, are you?"

The men just gaped.

Otto's underlings mocked, "Not live eels! Oh, no! They're using live eels? Nobody could be cruel enough to do that!"

"There's a law against that," Otto rumbled. "I think it carries the death penalty."

"What the hell's going on here?" a shaken fisherman demanded.

Otto stepped to the bow and looked back at the three bewildered faces. It then slammed down its left foot, then did so with the right, and repeated the sequence to make the boat rock as it started singing, "Rock-a-bye humans, on the boat top..."

"Otto's comrades joined the rocking, pulling down and up on the sides of the hapless vessel.

"When the sea swells, the bo-at will rock. When the bow breaks, the bo-at will sink, and down will fall you three assholes, into the drink! Ahahaha!"

The men sprawled on the deck. The boat's owner grabbed a gaff and swung it at Otto, who took the blow without even wincing.

"Now, why'd you do that?" it said, like an adult to a naughty child. Otto's arm shot out and grabbed him by the neck, tossing him like a rag doll, over its shoulder and into the water.

"Have at 'im, boys!"

Otto smiled tenderly and pointed suavely to one in particular. "...and girl." Its mate gave it a grotesque, love-struck, toothy "smile" before joining the shark-men, which had already ducked under. Suddenly, there was a wild thrashing at the spot in the water where the unlucky angler had landed. He managed to give out one extremely high-pitched, blood-curdling scream before they pulled him back down. The melee was so intense that water splashed into the boat. In the dim light from the bridge, the horrified men rose to their feet. They could see that the water was red with blood.

"Now, boys," Otto said in a matter-of-fact tone. "If you jump overboard and try to swim to shore, you're going to do one of the following: Choice A, you're going to make it; choice B, you're going to get torn to pieces by a type of shark that has yet to be '*discovered*'..." It uttered the word with contempt. "... by your rather delectable, though incredibly stupid, species. What's the answer? A or B?"

The two men were frozen. The commotion in the water suddenly died down, and the monsters grabbed the gunwales again, this time with bloody grins smeared across their maws, to watch Otto do its stuff.

"Wait a minute!" roared Otto, as it picked up the bucket of eels. "Oh, the humanity! They are using live eels! Angry crowd noises, comrades!"

The others obeyed, making grumbling, growling, hissing, and grunting sounds. Several turned their gruesome thumbs down. "To the lions!" one of them ululated.

"I'm afraid it doesn't look good, boys." Suddenly Otto's fists shot out in unison and smashed the jaws of the unlucky fishermen, who crumpled back to the deck. It dumped their tackle boxes, spilling the contents next to them as they writhed in pain. Otto chose the two largest fishhooks he could find, tied them in to the men's fishing lines, then grabbed one by the face while he pinned the other down with his knee.

"Now, you're gonna find out what it's like to be an eel used as bait!"

Otto plunged the hook through each man's eye sockets as they squirmed and slithered and shrieked. With one hand, it seized one of the unlucky anglers by the neck and tossed him over. The monster then let out the line, and laughed as it felt its "live bait" struggle at the other end.

Suddenly, its pole bent, and Otto cried, "I've got one—a big one!" The water roiled and splashed as the shark-beings attacked with glee. Otto held on to the pole, and tried reeling in the victim, laughing hysterically. Suddenly, the line snapped.

"No! He got away! He got away! I can't believe it! I had 'im," it mock-sobbed.

Otto rigged another hook to the line and pulled a struggling eel from the bucket. It shoved the eel in the last fisherman's face and asked, "So, how many times have you hooked eels through their eye sockets in the name of *sport*?"

Otto suddenly jammed the hook through the eel's eyes, the unlucky creature writhing in agony. "Do unto others as you would have them do unto you. Right?"

Otto fell on the remaining fisherman, pinning his arms down with its knees as it dangled the hooked eel over his grimacing face.

"Open wide!" Otto rumbled. The man was still conscious enough to clench his jaw and thrust his head from side to side as Otto's disciples popped up to watch their master doing what it did best.

"Bad boy!" growled the Karkarian. Rage suddenly distorted Otto's already distorted face, and it reached into the fisherman's mouth, yanking his jaw down until it snapped with a sickening crunch. Then, Otto shoved the eel into the angler's blood-filled mouth. The man's head gyrated like that of a hooked fish, spattering blood across the deck.

Otto's massive hand was completely inside the man's mouth as it concentrated on impaling the deepest part of the fisherman's tongue with the hook. The man gagged, and the eel's tail bolted down his gullet. Otto yanked hard, and the hook was set.

"Get outta my sight, Mister Sportsman," Otto snarled and then heaved him overboard, where the "comrades" immediately tore him to pieces.

"Watch out for bones and the hook!" Otto called. Then, like a child making sure that nobody was watching, Otto looked left, then right, lifting the bucket of eels to his yawning mouth and slurping them all down in one gulp.

"What the Christ is going on out there?" came a man's shout from the dark shore. Then, a flashlight stabbed the night.

"Time for dessert!" called Otto.

Chapter Twelve

Al Fergosi had to get all this out of his mind.

Out of my mind is right, he thought.

Both unable to sleep, Fergosi and Bob Brickley were at the Tuckernut substation at 6:00 a.m. They'd been able to reach the FBI, but the agents couldn't get there until that afternoon, and they didn't want to talk on the phone.

Brickley was on duty that day but, despite everything, it was Fergosi's day off, so he was dressed to fish. Hurricane Avril had turned slightly westward during the night, so a direct hit on southern New England was less likely, but it remained an enormous storm. Narragansett Bay was very choppy, and the wind was stiff.

Fergosi inspected the live eels slithering about in the tub at the back of Jon's Bait & Tackle in Jamestown. He looked over the selection of fishing lures, chose two, and then asked the grim-looking man behind the counter if he had any fresh bunker for sale. He did, and Fergosi bought six wide-eyed, bloody menhaden carcasses.

While paying, Fergosi asked the morose storekeeper, "What's the matter, Jon? Who died?" He meant it as a joke.

"I don't know, Al. Maybe four guys," the man answered.

Fergosi went pale.

"What?"

"You know how I stay open late most nights this time of year 'cause of the night fishing? Well, last night, three guys in a brand new cuddy pull up to the dock in the back to buy some bait. When they leave, they go right down there to Potter Cove. I watched their lights." He pointed out the window at the uneasy bay.

"Don't tell me..." Fergosi froze.

"Yeah, they never came back. And there's Pete Petrov, who lives on the shore down there. They found pools of blood on the rocks behind his house this morning. He's gone, too."

Fergosi stared out the window, his head shaking back and forth, mouth open. He saw two police boats and a Coast

Guard "41" patrol boat prowling back and forth across the West Passage. Another vessel anchored in the water, with several divers on the deck, preparing their equipment.

"This is bad. This is a shitstorm!" Fergosi muttered.

"I guess it is. At first, I didn't think this was tied in with the guys that disappeared down your way. I don't think that, anymore," the storekeeper replied.

"What about their boat?"

"They found it piled up on the rocks on the Newport side. Blood all over it."

"Christ!" Fergosi started pacing back and forth. "Where's the boat now, Jon?"

"Your brother cops have it. And Leo at the Narragansett Bay Dive Shop, did you hear?"

"No, what?" Fergosi was paler than ever.

"They lost a diver at the U-boat, yesterday. Just disappeared. Gone."

A look between puzzled and frightened crossed the man's face.

"You know, Al, most people around here think it's this pirate shit, like goes on in the Caribbean. They attack boats, kill everybody, repaint the thing, and use it for smugglin'."

"That happens out on the water in the middle of nowhere, and they don't trash the boat," Fergosi noted.

"That's right. So, this makes me think of a story a customer told me a few weeks back. At the time, I thought it was hysterical. Now, I'm not so sure."

"What did he say, Jon?"

"He said he was in a boat, bottom fishing off Beavertail Point down here, when he had a strike. He yanked back but didn't set the hook. So, he reeled his line in to see if the bait was still on. It wasn't. What was on the hook was a *note* on that waterproof paper they have!"

Fergosi listened very carefully. "A note? That said what?"

The man glanced at a father and his two young sons as they entered the store.

"Well, I won't repeat the language," he murmured, nodding toward the boys, who were goggling over the display of lures. "Let's just say it was a two-word cuss. I figured it must be some diver playing a joke, but this guy said he saw no air bubbles. He was totally freaked out, and I laughed at him."

The storekeeper shook his head. "I can't shake the feeling.

Maybe, this guy had a brush with whatever the hell is behind all these disappearances." He stepped over to the window and looked out at the police and Coast Guard vessels. "I feel it, Al. There's somethin' very, very wrong about all this."

"Me, too," Fergosi murmured.

He paid for his bait and lures. As he left, the storekeeper bid him "good luck". Fergosi felt that the man might as well have said, "Just make it through this alive." As Fergosi pulled out of the parking lot, a car with two male occupants discreetly followed him, who didn't realize that they weren't the only ones tailing the off-duty cop.

Fergosi dropped by a grocery store to buy a snack. Standing in the checkout line, he glanced at the local newspapers, wondering if the most recent issues, many of whose cover photos showed Bob Brickley in the Tuckernut security Jeep with words like "Hero" and "He saved my life!" blazing at the top of the fold, were still on the racks.

They weren't. With follow-up stories, the daily papers were still getting mileage out of the shark attacks at Tuckernut Beach from three days before. There were more spectacular shots of the attack in progress, then a shot of the two babes who'd managed to get out alive, including that cute lifeguard. They were the newest heroes. Brickley was yesterday's news. Then, Fergosi noticed another headline toward the bottom of the page.

"'Heroe's attacker a ninety-five-pound dog, police say."

Fergosi shook his head and smiled. "Well, that didn't take long to leak out," he muttered. He bought the paper, only to find another small story, this one about the State Police and their "promising leads" to the identity of the "shark-costumed" figure at the Titanic Café. There was a longer story about the continued, fruitless search for the missing Tuckernut fishermen.

Fergosi, of course, knew differently. While he was passionate about fishing, he couldn't help thinking of the horrible deaths so many of his fellow anglers had suffered in recent days. He shivered.

If it wasn't daylight, I'd be headed inland.

Nevertheless, his service revolver was right where he could reach it.

Fergosi found his favorite spot unoccupied—a sheltered inlet with a tiny beach along the rocky shore of the bay. He'd discovered the place the previous year while snorkeling. It was a peaceful place where the water was less than twenty feet deep, with a sandy bottom among a jumble of glacial boulders. It was perfect for bottom fishing and not getting your hook snagged on a rock. While this was far from the best time of day to fish here, Fergosi just wanted to enjoy the peace. He realized, of course, that wasn't about to happen on this day. As it was, the storm winds were increasing, and peace was becoming a rare commodity in southern Rhode Island lately.

This spot also offered superb bird-watching, and Fergosi set his binocular case gently on the sand next to him. He unfolded his folding canvas seat and arranged his fishing gear. He scaled a bunker before cutting it into chunks—scaling it made it much easier to set the hook into the weak, often crumbling flesh—baited his line, stood to aim for the sandy spot offshore, and delicately cast his line. Direct hit.

Making himself comfortable, Fergosi had a pretty good idea of where the two men who'd been following him were staked out. What he didn't know was that he had a third tail.

Roughly a hundred yards away, among the rocks, a powerful pair of binoculars was trained on Al Fergosi. Flash Swynecock had a hunch, and he and Lance Grebe had decided to stick with Fergosi all day, just to see what would happen. They had a feeling that whatever it was, it would be soon.

Behind a thicket of shrubs, separated from the shore by the immense, meticulously groomed summer home of some multi-millionaire, was Fergosi's former high school teacher-turned-stalker. He'd left his slingshot at home. In his hand was a .44 caliber revolver. He silently cursed himself for buying a handgun.

"The most powerful handgun in the world," says Dirty Harry, Frank Slade thought bitterly.

What the hell made me buy a .44 instead of a rifle and scope? At this distance, it'll be a miracle.

He'd have to get closer before he began blasting the fucker. Then, he swore quietly as that same itch from under his neck brace returned with a vengeance.

* * * *

Glancing out the window of the Tuckernut substation's interrogation room, Bob Brickley could see the end of the street and the Atlantic Ocean beyond. He knew that his erstwhile acquaintance "Bob" was out there. The fact that the "enforcer" hadn't shown up off West Beach the previous night sent a chill through him.

I don't know what scares me more. Meeting "Bob" or not meeting "Bob", Brickley thought.

From the window, he observed that the sea was jumbled and frothy, and sightseers packed the overlook taking in the spectacle of enormous rollers breaking over the rocks. They half hoped to get a look at the famous Tuckernut shark. The normally blue-green sea was an angry brown, speckled with rafts of white and ocher foam. To the west, just behind the Watch Hill Lighthouse, lightning flickered from the dark clouds.

Brickley himself was quite a sight. He fidgeted in an uncomfortable wooden chair, fresh bandages around his head protecting his nationally famous right ear, which still throbbed.

On the desk before him, a life-sized model of Fritz's toothy jaws perched menacingly on the desk. FBI agent John Kelwin and State Police Detective Rick Angell stood on either side of the desk, arms folded, gazing down on the village security guard. Brickley's revised statement of what happened to his ear, and its non-relation to the Titanic Café incident, was thoroughly documented on paper, in digital audio and video, and, apparently, in the newspapers.

"Our apologies, Mister Brickley, for leaking this information to the media," Kelwin stated. "But it was actually helpful. It's important that people concentrate on that story and not continue to speculate on something that could cause a panic."

When he'd told his story—his complete story—Brickley was more surprised at the reaction of these cops than at Fergosi's. Brickley had provided very full and complete information, right down to the waitress mistakenly serving Patti Shipley's margarita to Joya Wolf at the Titanic, to trying to pull up his pants while cornered by Fritz in the bathroom, to Patti's look of horror the split second before Brickley unleashed his stomach contents all over her bedroom. Right down to his encounter with "Bob".

In the end, though, Fergosi—his new friend—had been right: The FBI knew something about the Karkarians, though they wouldn't say exactly how much. They had also known for a very long time. This Kelwin even seemed disappointed that Brickley had blown it as a liaison with "the enforcer" on the first day.

"We could have used a local contact," Angell admitted. "But we have to stick with stories about dogs and shark costumes for now. You are not to talk about this with anyone, do you understand? That includes Miss Shipley."

"Why can't I tell Patti?" Brickley asked. "She's a brave and responsible person, and she works for the town! She might be able to help! People will be dying!"

"That'll be all for now, Mister Brickley," Kelwin stated.

"Is this where the attack—the feeding frenzy—will come? You're talking to Al Fergosi later today, right?" Brickley almost pleaded.

"Thank you, Mister Brickley."

* * * *

Frightened and depressed, Brickley wandered out of the station, got into his Jeep, and drove down the street toward the water. He pulled over to stare at the jumbled, foamy breakers.

Why should I even care? Maybe I should move. Maybe to Missouri or somewhere.

A number of gawkers recognized Brickley, but the looks they gave him weren't the admiring ones he'd become used to in recent days.

How are the mighty fallen! Brickley thought, remembering the Bible passage from his Sunday school days.

It was then that the call came.

"Bob? This is Donna Cardoza at the mayor's office. I'm sorry to have to tell you this, but the mayor said to tell you that you're suspended for a month without pay until your case can be reviewed."

"What case?"

"It's all this media crap, Bob. Don't ask me. Please return the Jeep, your uniform, and equipment to the police station at once. Somebody will be in touch."

"What the hell am I supposed to do, Donna? Walk home in my underpants?"

Click.

"What the fuck else can go wrong, today?" he shouted to

nobody in particular as he swung the wheel and headed back up toward the station. "Next thing I'll see is sharks running down the street!"

Fifteen minutes later, he was hoofing it home—uniform, German binoculars, and all. Suddenly, he heard a car horn and turned to see Henry "Hulk" Hoagland, Joya Wolf, and Patti Shipley, bandages and all, in Shipley's red Mustang convertible.

"Hey!" Shipley called above the steady roar of the sea. "Where's your Jeep?"

"Hey," Brickley droned glumly. "I just got suspended."

There was a chorus of groans and "those bastards" from the car.

Meanwhile, the gawkers were close enough to see who was in the car, and they came running.

"Oh, God. No!" cried Shipley as she looked back. "Quick, Brickley. Jump in!"

They tore away from the curb as cell phone cameras clicked, and they headed along Shore Road.

"Close one! We were hoping to enjoy the day. Beaches are closed because of the shark and the surf," Shipley said. She wanted to kiss him. As Brickley glanced over his shoulder at the disappearing mob, he noticed that Wolf and Hulk were holding hands in the back seat. Brickley was happy for Wolf but noticed that the smile on her face seemed distant and almost sad as she looked at him.

"How're you guys doing?" Brickley asked.

"To be honest," answered Shipley, "All those damn stitches! I'm sore as hell."

Thanks to you, I know the feeling, Brickley thought.

"Yeah, me too," said Wolf, her voice barely audible above the tumult of the wind and the waves to their right.

"We should call ourselves the 'bandage club'," said Brickley with a sardonic smile. He raised his binoculars and scanned the seaward horizon, watching the intrepid Block Island Ferry kick up spray as it emerged from behind the Watch Hill Lighthouse. It rolled and yawed its way through the heavy seas. He couldn't believe it was still sailing in this weather.

"Wow!" Brickley blurted.

"What?" asked Shipley.

"The ferry just got hit by lightning! But it's still chugging along," he called over the wind.

"I hope nobody was on deck!" Hulk shouted. Suddenly, "Patti, stop! Bob, give me those binoculars!"

Hulk jumped out of the car and held the binoculars to his eyes. "There's somebody out in the water, just offshore!"

The rest jumped out, and they all ran to the rocks. "There he is!" called Shipley. "He's got to be in trouble! He's gonna smash into the rocks!"

But the buck-naked, seven-foot human form picked its way quite skillfully through the pounding waves and the boulders. It reached the rocks and looked up at the four gaping forms above, exposing them to his donkey-hung nakedness. He pointed at Brickley and shouted in a rumbling, unearthly voice above the roar of the sea, "I've got a message for you!"

Against his better judgment, Brickley picked his way down the slippery rocks to the dripping, naked giant as the other three gazed disbelievingly. Also gaping were two FBI agents assigned to watch the coast from a motel room about 500 yards up the road.

"Oh, my God!" cried Wolf, turning pale. "That looks just like the guy at the Titanic that turned into a shark!"

Hulk and Shipley just stared at her, then looked back to the rocks.

The giant gestured excitedly toward the ferry. Brickley's three friends could only catch the first few words.

"How did you know where I was?" Brickley asked nervously.

"Never mind that!" the man roared, then dropped his voice.

In another minute, Brickley was climbing hurriedly back to his friends while, to their astonishment, the giant plunged back into the water and didn't surface.

"What the Christ was that about?" Hulk cried, still staring at the point where the man had disappeared.

"Hulk, give me your cell phone!"

"What's wrong with yours?"

"I think it's being monitored."

"What?" the huge lifeguard blurted, but he handed over the phone.

Brickley dialed Fergosi's number as all four ran back to the car.

"Al?" Brickley called into the phone.

"I ain't here. You know what to do and when to do it," Fergosi's recorded voice barked back.

A Little Night Fishing

"Shit! When you're done fishing, call me, and I mean right now! No time to explain!"

He jabbed the "end" button, then got another idea.

"Patti! Drop me off, then go home and get your roommate's shotgun and as many shells as possible!"

She stared at him, then started the car and roared off toward his apartment, a few blocks inland.

"Hulk, Joya. Either of you have guns?" Both shook their heads, now thoroughly mystified.

"Why don't you just call the National Guard?" Hulk shouted over the wind.

"I should call the FBI, but I don't know how much they know. They wouldn't tell me. Maybe, they won't believe me, and I'll just get myself in more trouble. No time! This I have to do myself!" Brickley hollered back, leaving the others more bewildered than ever.

"He's really gone this time," Hulk muttered to Joya. Then to Brickley, "Who—and what—the hell was that guy in the water, Bob?"

"I thought he wouldn't talk to me again, but I guess he had second thoughts," Brickley called back.

"What?"

* * * *

Brickley burst into his apartment, grabbed the local directory, and then lurched to the phone. The other three trickled in behind him. He tore several pages while trying to find the number for the Block Island Ferry's office. He dialed it, identified himself and, to the consternation of the others, reported that the ferry was in danger, and might have a bomb onboard.

He was told that the ferry's radio wasn't working.

"That's right," Brickley shouted into the phone. "I saw it get hit by lightning! You have to get in touch with the captain—the guy must have a cell phone! Call the Coast Guard and tell them to get a helicopter out, with some sharpshooters!"

The woman at the other end was flummoxed. Brickley slammed the receiver and prayed for his cell phone to ring, monitored or not.

"C'mon, Fergosi! Call me!"

As if on cue, the phone blared.

Brickley punched the "answer" button and bellowed,

"They're going after the ferry!"

"Oh, shit!" Fergosi cried.

"I saw 'Bob'! He said one of 'Otto's' gang squealed. He says they've laid a minefield in the ferry's course!"

"Bob?" Hulk squeaked.

"Jesus!" cried Fergosi. "Did you alert the ferry company?"

"Yeah! Lightning knocked out the ferry's radio! But I don't know if they believed me, anyway!"

"You didn't mention talking sharks, did you?" After a brief pause, Fergosi said, "I know what I'm gonna' do! Look, I'm going out after the ferry!"

"How?" Brickley shouted.

"Just meet me at the Breachway Slips!"

Brickley flew out the door and bolted for his vehicle—a yellow 1998 Geo Metro with a black convertible top. His neighbors all called it "the bumble bee".

Just then, Shipley's Mustang screeched into the driveway, and she struggled out, groaning because of her sore body.

"Did you get the gun?" Brickley called back as he ran.

"Yes! And a bunch of shells!"

"Get back in your car and follow me!"

Groaning again, Shipley eased back into the Mustang and slammed the door. Hulk jumped in behind her, but Wolf shouted, "I'll go with Bobby!" and leaped into the Geo's passenger seat. Brickley and Wolf tore out of the driveway and toward Tuckernut Breachway.

"I didn't think that roller skate could carry two people!" Hulk called to Shipley over the wind.

In a few minutes, they saw Brickley jam to a halt along the Breachway Slips—a boat launching area with floating docks and about thirty large powerboats and sailing vessels. He and Wolf ran up to the chain-link fence and the gate, which was open. Shipley parked, and she and Hulk ran up to Brickley and Wolf, who were looking about wildly.

"Can you see Fergosi?" Brickley called to the others.

"No more than you can," Hulk replied over the tearing wind. "I know for a fact that he doesn't own a boat."

"Shit!" Brickley spat. "Then, what did he want us to meet him here for?"

Before anybody could stop him, Brickley started springing from boat to boat. A few owners were on their decks, securing their vessels for the approaching storm. Though, there seemed to be nobody aboard the more powerful boats, the kind they'd need to get out to the ferry in time.

"What are you doing, now?" Shipley hollered.

"Trying to find somebody to take us out, or at least a boat with keys in it!" Brickley called back.

"What moron is going to leave keys..." Hulk shouted.

Brickley was slumping over in despair. "We need to take a boat out and stop that ferry. They have to be contacted!"

The four of them stood together, and Hulk finally blurted. "Brickley, it's time to tell us what the hell this is all about!"

Then, all four heads turned to the sound of a huge powerboat, throbbing over the gale. Around the bend, like a glistening black god, came a thirty-foot cigarette boat. It was none other than *Shot Baker*.

"This is too good to be true!" Brickley shouted as he sprinted to the end of the dock and waved frantically. In his jacket pocket, he felt the weight of his father's gun, which had somehow survived that seaborne encounter with the "enforcer".

If they don't buy my impounding their boat, then I'll have to use the gun! I just hope they've been out in that beauty all morning and didn't hear about me getting fired. And I hope they have gas!

The boat accelerated slightly and pointed its raked, razor-sharp bow toward him. As it neared, Brickley saw two occupants, both clad in black wet-suits, giving them a classical, evil appearance.

"What's up, young man?" the driver called in a somewhat familiar voice.

Brickley was surprised to notice that here were a man and woman well beyond retirement age. Then, he noticed a modified pet carrier bolted to the deck next to the woman, and inside it was a white miniature poodle.

"Tuckernut Village security," he called. I need to commandeer your craft, sir. Don't worry. There's nothing to be afraid of."

Christ! I hope they don't know that a security guard can't impound their boat!

The two elderly people grinned. That wasn't how Brickley expected them to react. Their faces lit up with recognition.

"Hey, you're that boy I've called the rescue squad on twice!" the man yelled. "Are they coming along, too?" he asked, nodding toward Hulk, Wolf, and Shipley. The two seniors seemed totally unfazed by the fact that Patti Shipley was clutching a shotgun.

Who are these people? Brickley wondered.

"Uh, yes, sir," he answered. It finally dawned on him that these two were the ones forever walking their poodle along the sidewalk above the beach.

Sheltered somewhat from the worst winds and waves in this place, the powerful boat purred like a tiger as it drifted toward the dock.

"We had a feeling there was trouble brewing," the old man said, nodding to Patti and her shotgun. "Maybe, we can help you out."

"Yes, sir. I do believe you can. And thank you!" Brickley responded firmly.

"Is anybody besides this pretty young lady packin'?" he asked Brickley.

"I am," he declared.

As the boat reached the dock, the man gently put it into reverse, making the vessel come to a skillful stop less than a foot from the edge.

"Those two don't have weapons?"

Brickley looked at Hulk and Wolf. "No, sir."

"Well, climb on in, and then I may be able to help those two out. What do you need the weapons for?"

What the hell? Brickley thought.

"We have information that...terrorists...are about the attack the Block Island Ferry. Her radio's out, so nobody can contact her, and cell phone info is uncertain. So, we need to get out there."

The seniors glanced at each other with sparkling eyes.

The four friends piled in, and the poodle began yapping.

"It's all right, Ike," the wet-suit clad woman cooed. "They're not pirates!"

"I'm Arnie, and this is my wife of forty-five years, Dora-Mae."

Dora-Mae smiled and called, "Welcome aboard!"

"A pleasure to be aboard," Brickley answered clumsily, not believing his luck that they believed him. "This has gas?"

"Just filled up!" Arnie replied.

Brickley introduced his three friends, who nodded with great unease as Arnie backed away from the dock and turned toward the frothing ocean.

"You'd better batten down," he called. "It's pretty rough out there. I hope you don't get seasick!"

The four friends glanced at each other, then noticed that the comfortable, red leather seats all had seat belts. They buckled in as they reach the rough water. Arnie gunned the throttle, and *Shot Baker* roared forward, taking the first big wave like a ski jump. Shipley and Wolf screamed. Brickley and Hulk just gritted their teeth and held on.

Arnie hollered over the wind. "I don't suppose you have any ID, Mister Guard with no authority to impound anything!"

Brickley swallowed. "Uh...I left it back at the police station just now."

Absolutely true.

"I'm sorry about all this, Arnie, but the danger to the ferry is real! We need to get to the ferry!"

"Okay!" Arnie yelled.

Taking it all in stride, Dora-Mae tried to make reassuring conversation.

"This is Eisenhower," she shouted, introducing the highly agitated poodle. "But we call him 'Ike'."

Brickley glanced at the little dog, hunkered down in his cage. The pooch was shaking and drooling profusely, as if it knew that a predator wasn't far away. Brickley noticed a laminated photograph of a burly, orange cat attached to the cage.

"You have a cat, too?" Brickley asked, trying to calm himself.

"At the house we just bought here, yes. But he stays home. Cats don't like the water," Dora-Mae yelled as Brickley watched the poodle shiver with fear.

"We also raise chickens, ducks, and guinea fowl. They all eat ticks, 'specially guineas," the lady continued.

Brickley blinked. "Here?"

"No, not here," she responded. "Back where we're from. Chatham County, North Carolina. Close to Siler City. Y'know, where Aunt Bea is from." Dora-Mae pronounced the word as "ant".

Ant Bee? thought Brickley.

"I guess you're too young for Mayberry." She laughed.

Brickley had no idea what she was talking about.

Meanwhile, things had actually gotten smoother. *Shot Baker* was at the perfect speed to skim the wave tops. In the distance, the heaving white bulk of the Block Island Ferry came within sight, though headed away from them. Arnie aimed straight for her.

It was then that lightning, of a sort, hit Joya Wolf. Her heart and mind were suddenly struck with the cold realization that she wasn't coming back from this trip. It hit her all at once, like a waking dream. At first, instead of fear, she felt something like relief. She remembered screaming like a coward instead of helping Brickley as he and the wacko wrestled that night in the Titanic Café's parking lot.

And I was going to kill Patti Shipley. Kill her! My new friend!

This haunted Wolf constantly.

Am I really a loser—a coward? No! I am not a coward! And now, I'll redeem myself.

Wolf's gaze fixed itself on the still-distant ferry. Then, it really hit her. *Holy shit…I'm gonna' die!*

Just as suddenly, Arnie called, "Mister Guard, can you drive a boat?"

"I guess so," Brickley responded.

"Okay, just take the wheel and hold her steady!"

Brickley took the wheel, and the man disappeared down a hatch.

Must have to pee, Brickley thought.

But that wasn't what Arnie was doing. In another minute, he emerged from the hatch. Strapped over his shoulders were two mean-looking, semi-automatic rifles, and in his hands were two more. He wore a heavy backpack that Brickley guessed was full of ammunition. The four passengers watched with open mouths. Dora-Mae grinned. Brickley just tried to hold the boat steady. The ferry drew ever nearer.

Christ! They're drug smugglers! Brickley thought.

Arnie motioned to Hulk. The big lifeguard unbuckled himself and eased over unsteadily.

"This is for you." Arnie unslung a rifle and handed it to Hulk. "Know anything about guns?"

Before answering, Hulk checked to see that the rifle's chamber was unloaded or "clear"—standard procedure for anyone who does know about guns.

"Four years in the Army, sir. Two tours in Iraq."

"Good man! Still, my dear Hulk, you've probably never seen one of these. It's a 7.62-millimeter M14 rifle, used by the Army in Vietnam until 1970. This magazine holds thirty rounds of good old .308 Winchester ammo." He handed Hulk the weapon and the black, rectangular container.

Hulk went back to his seat with a wry smile on his face.

"Now, Joya," Arnie yelled, handing her another M14 and a magazine. "Take this over to Hulk, and he'll explain it to you."

"Thank you, sir, but he doesn't have to explain it. I belong to the Tuckernut Rod and Gun Club. I hunt, and I've won fourteen shooting competitions."

"Well, done, young lady!" Arnie replied. Then, he turned to Brickley, who was still gripping the boat's wheel.

"Kid, you brought the right people!"

When Wolf sat back down, Dora-Mae looked at her approvingly. "So, you know about firearms."

"Yes," Wolf answered, swallowing a lump of nervousness. "I've even fired an M-1A before."

Arnie overheard, and he and Dora-Mae were openly impressed. Wolf could become the daughter they'd never had, but the sea spray was flying in the wind.

"Aren't you afraid of exposing these babies to the salt water?" Wolf asked while her hand lovingly stroked the rifle's receiver.

"Oh, Arnie's got more. Guns are one of his hobbies, but having fun target shootin' with 'em in all types of weather is more important than keeping 'em in museum-quality condition," she laughed.

Dora-Mae looked at Brickley and called, "So, you see, we're not drug smugglers."

Brickley went cold. *Christ! They're psychic, too!*

They were only about a mile from the ferry, and the sea was rougher than ever.

"Dora-Mae and I met the hard way during the Vietnam War," Arnie called. "I was a Navy 'Swift Boat' driver, and she was an Army nurse. I was hit while patrolling the Mekong Delta, and Dora-Mae saved my life."

Wolf smiled, but all four young people were speechless. Ike was urinating.

All at once, Arnie yelled, "I'll take the wheel, kid! Go buckle in!"

The instant Brickley did so, *Shot Baker* charged over a huge swell and became airborne. Everyone felt weightless and held on. Then, with a hollow *wump* and a cloud of spray, the boat slammed back into the sea, the weightlessness becoming back-buckling g-forces. Brickley felt nauseous.

"You'd better put these on," Dora-Mae hollered, opening a hatch and pulling out life vests.

The four young people looked downright frightened.

"Nothing puts things into perspective like the ocean, especially when it's wild," Dora-Mae called. "Which reminds me," she added, pulling out some nylon webbing. "Tie yourselves in. Then, you can stand up and fire without getting thrown overboard."

She demonstrated on Hulk. Between swells, she clipped a harness tightly around his waist, then tied a length of nylon webbing to it. She attached the other end to a bar running along the gunwales.

The average swell was now six feet.

"Time for the hoods!" Arnie yelled to Dora-Mae. They both pulled the black wet-suit hoods over their heads and strapped goggles over their eyes. "I hope you kids are ready to get wet!"

With the coast receding quickly behind them, Joya Wolf silently said good-bye.

Chapter Thirteen

Al Fergosi pulled up to the Breachway Slips just as *Shot Baker* roared around the jetty and out to sea.

"Where's Brickley?" he muttered to himself, his gaze darting from boat to boat. There had to be owners here somewhere, securing their boats for the storm.

Can't wait! One of these has to have somebody on board or at least keys! he thought, fighting desperation.

He could call his on-duty comrades and the harbor patrol, but they must have their hands full with storm preparations. Who knew how long it would take simply to get through, and would they even believe him?

When somethin' has to be done right, do it yourself!

Fergosi darted from boat to boat. Spotting a backpack and some fishing gear on a twenty-five-foot cabin cruiser named *Motion of the Ocean*, he jumped aboard and rifled through the pack, and he found keys.

"Hey, what are you doing?" hollered a voice from the porthole of a neighboring sailboat.

"Taking this boat!" Fergosi shouted back. "What are you doing?"

"I'm calling the police!"

"Thank God! Tell them the Block Island Ferry is heading for a minefield right now, and that Sergeant Fergosi is going to try and stop it!"

Fergosi leaped to the wheel and jammed a likely-looking key into the ignition. With a burst of blue smoke, the engine sprang to life. He scrambled along the deck and frantically un-cleated the vessel from its moorings. Then, he backed out of the slip, shifted, and hit the throttle. *Motion of the Ocean* lurched forward.

Fergosi added more power, and the boat thundered into the Breachway to an angry shout of, "Hey! Holy shit!" from a bearded man running down the dock. Evidently, this was the boat's owner.

Gritting his teeth and with butterflies churning inside

him, Fergosi aimed the cruiser's bow toward the open ocean, three minutes away at top speed, and pushed the throttle as far as it would go. He had some powerboat experience, but never at driving a boat through seas like he saw ahead.

Fergosi's stomach knotted as he watched a wall of spray burst over the jetty. He realized that he was trembling all over.

"Don't move!" A shaky voice suddenly commanded from the cabin hatch. Fergosi glanced to his left to see a slender man in his early twenties, wearing only bathing trunks, pointing a Beretta 9-millimeter automatic at his head.

* * * *

Flash Swynecock and Lance Grebe jumped out of their car at the Breachway Slips and immediately saw Fergosi's pickup truck parked askew in the lot. They knew that something big must be up out on the water. The two men headed onto the docks. Behind Grebe, Swynecock lugged his camera and prodigious beer belly. They labored up and down the docks, looking for a boat to rent or, if necessary, steal. Flash spotted a woman and two young teenage girls tying something down aboard a small cabin cruiser named *Fair & Square*.

"There!" Swynecock barked, motioning with his chin. He and Grebe walked over as fast as they could and jumped aboard.

"Hey, who do you think you are..." the startled woman began.

"We're the ones renting this boat," Swynecock called.

"What the hell? You're renting shit! I'm calling the cops."

She yanked a cell phone from the clip on her belt and started to dial. She dropped the phone and screamed as Grebe suddenly grabbed her by the back of her pants and threw her onto the dock. Flash went after the now-screaming children and heaved each one of them off the boat and onto the dock.

Aboard a few nearby boats, heads poked out of hatches.

"Hey!" called one man from a sailboat three slips away.

But *Fair & Square*'s keys were in the ignition. Grebe fired up the engine while Swynecock untied the boat. They sped into the Breachway as people ran down the docks.

* * * *

From the nearby parking lot, a crazed-looking man with a neck brace watched Fergosi, then the photographer, make their moves. A bandana covered his lower face, like some Wild West bandit about to rob a stagecoach. He saw several people on a dock, comforting a woman and two kids. With everyone agitated and looking toward that scene, Frank Slade ran forward and put his weapon against the head of a man standing next to a thirty-foot cruiser, *Holy Mackerel VI*.

"Don't turn around," Slade commanded. "Just hand over the keys!"

With shaking hands, the man did so.

"Now, untie it!" Slade ordered. The terrified man did so without a word. Then Slade, in his turn, roared out the Breachway and into the open sea.

One open-mouthed boat owner gazed after *Holy Mackerel VI* and cried, "What the hell's going on here, today?"

* * * *

Back aboard *Motion of the Ocean*, it was more of a squeal than an order. "Stop the boat now, or I'll fire!"

Fergosi peered ahead and estimated twenty more seconds until they hit the ocean swells.

The man darted up the steps and stood, his feet splayed apart, behind Fergosi, with a gun aimed at his back.

"I'm a police sergeant," Fergosi shouted. "There's a public emergency, and I'm commandeering this boat!"

"I don't care if you're a Jedi Knight! Stop right now!"

"I'm a police sergeant, damn it, and I've got to get to the Block Island Ferry!"

"With this boat in that ocean?" The man was aghast.

This guy must be a fruitcake, he thought.

"Then, definitely stop this boat and get away from the controls, or I'll enthusiastically shoot you to pieces!"

Fergosi watched the turbulence at the mouth of the Breachway come closer and closer.

Anytime now.

"I said now!" screamed the man as he realized they were about to hit the swells.

Fergosi noted the precise location, looked at the gun pointing at his nose, then said, "Okay, I'll do as you say."

He slammed the throttle to neutral. The bow hit the first

swell, the boat lurched to a complete stop, and the young man flew across the deck, smashing face-first into the steps leading to the tiny forward deck. The gun flew out of the man's hand and skidded across the deck to Fergosi's feet. He picked it up, checked the safety, then shoved the weapon into his belt.

Fergosi drew his military-issue 45-millimeter automatic and pointed it at the guy's profusely bleeding nose. "Sit on that bench, and keep your hands where I can see them!"

"Do as he says, Brad!" Fergosi was startled to hear the anguished voice of a woman over the roar of wind and wave. She emerged from the cabin and onto the heaving deck wearing a blue sweat suit, and helped the man up.

"Oww," he groaned.

"Ma'am, I really am a police officer," Fergosi told her. Still holding his weapon, he pulled his badge out of his back pocket and flashed it. She and Brad stared.

"Now, please sit on the bench and don't move, ma'am. You," Fergosi motioned to the man. "Grab us three life jackets. People are about to be killed, and I need this boat to stop it!"

"What do you mean?" the women squeaked, almost in a panic. Fergosi didn't answer.

All three, with the woman sobbing and Brad still groaning, put on the life vests.

Fergosi gunned the engine and plunged farther into the enraged Atlantic. He cursed as the vessel lurched upward over an eight-foot swell, then plunged into the trough. He spun the wheel, swinging the bow at the slight angle necessary to meet the next swell without swamping or capsizing.

To the anguished cries of his "passengers", the bow heaved skyward again, then slid down the wave's back, but without burying the bow in the next swell. Meanwhile, Fergosi's feet and his passengers' buttocks were suddenly suspended in the air, only to slap back down, the g-forces slamming Brad's and his companion's faces against their own laps, and he cried out with fresh pain. Walls of spray burst over the boat like shotgun blasts, and within seconds, everyone was soaked and shivering.

As *Motion of the Ocean* heaved to the crest of another swell, Fergosi spotted the ferry. It seemed far away. Only then did he think to check to fuel gauge. It was close to empty.

"Shit! Shit! Shit! How far can we get in this thing on less than an eighth of a tank of gas?" he called back to the passengers, who were on their knees clutching a deck bench with both arms.

"We could get back to the slips," Brad called miserably, his voice muffled behind a bloodied towel.

Fergosi kept the bow pointed at an intercept angle to the ferry.

"One of you get on the radio and send out an S.O.S. Tell them the situation on this boat, that the Block Island Ferry is heading into a mine field laid by terrorists, and that their radio is out."

"I'll do it," cried the girl, "and you can call me Margot." Then, "Look out!"

Fergosi saw it at that instant—a monster swell with a tumbling whitecap. It was about to slam into the boat's side from a slightly different angle than the others. He spun the wheel again, bringing the bow into the breaking wave. The collision threw Margot and Brad against the gunwales while Fergosi shot off his seat and smashed into the control panel. Seawater crashed over the boat, virtually knocking it onto its side. Thrown back into his seat, Fergosi frantically slammed the wheel in the other direction to keep the boat from rolling any further. Another wave slapped *Motion of the Ocean* hard to port. As the bow hurtled upward once more, Fergosi's gaze pointed directly at a wild display of lightning shooting from very dark, low clouds right before them.

* * * *

"Jesus, boss. We can't keep going in this!" Grebe gasped as *Fair & Square* tossed and yawed in the swells. "I've already lost the cop in the other boat, because the fuckin' waves are too big to see over!"

"Keep going, damn it!" shouted Swynecock. "That cop is on to something big, and I want to shoot it! I'm on a roll, and I'm taking you with me, Lance. We're already famous! Let's do this! We're talkin' immortality, man! Margaret Bourke White, Robert Capa, and Flash Swynecock!"

The idea of fame made the seas seem a little more manageable to Grebe. He hit the throttle, and within twenty seconds, the first ten-foot swell slammed into the bow.

* * * *

"I'll fuckin' kill him! I'll fuckin' kill him! Yahh! Kill him! Ahh!" The now completely unhinged driving instructor felt his neck injury register every jolt as *Holy Mackerel VI* plunged up and down through the waves. Frank Slade aimed his hijacked craft in the direction he'd last seen Fergosi's cabin cruiser, and did his best to hold that course.

"If I can't shoot him, I'll fuckin' ram him!" Slade bellowed to the wind.

* * * *

In their black wet-suits and with their Vietnam-era weapons slung on their backs, Arnie and Dora-Mae were as happy as clams, while the four others were soaked and shivering, fighting back nausea and terror. Little Ike remained frozen, his four legs splayed out so much that his stomach was less than an inch above the bottom of his cage.

Shot Baker was in the maelstrom, with white froth and heaving swells coming from two directions. Their guns and ammo were soaked. Several wondered if the weapons would work at all.

Now tied down, Bob Brickley scoured the near horizon for the ferry, but could see only walls of water under the darkening skies.

Suddenly, *Shot Baker* landed on the crest of one of the swells, which were now growing too large for the powerful vessel to skim. And there before them was the white, rust-streaked hull of the elderly ferry as it swayed along, the far-off sand cliffs of Block Island barely visible through the rain and mist beyond. He noticed that Arnie was cruising along at a perfect intercept angle, and they were making excellent time. When they slid down the back of the wave into the trough, all Brickley could see were walls of water rearing up on every side, and they might as well have been completely alone on the insane sea.

* * * *

From the crest of a foamy swell, with its only functioning eye, Otto spotted one of two approaching powerboats that it and its cohorts, less one, had been listening to for the past several minutes. Where the other Karkarian had disappeared to, Otto didn't know or care. It assumed that it had panicked and fled at the last moment. It also noted that the ferry was heading straight toward the minefield, and should reach its outer boundary in less than ten minutes. In fact, Otto was very pleased with the way things were going. The two other approaching "cans of meat" were a bonus. On top of that, Otto and its cronies had been able to salvage seventeen mines from the sunken U-boat—not the six they had expected.

The more, the merrier! Otto thought cheerfully as it spotted yet another motorboat coming from almost the opposite angle as the first.

The depths throbbed with the sound of the ferry's screw, and the higher-pitched whine of the other approaching propellers was like the aroma of a barbecued steak to someone with a huge appetite.

Otto also got the feeling that one of the motorboats was about to reach the outer boundary of the minefield.

There'll be nothing but scraps left over after that small boat hits one of those huge mines, Otto thought sadly.

* * * *

Motion of the Ocean dodged one swell, only to have its bow facing directly into another, coming from an oblique angle. The boat was punched to a virtual stop as the crest of the wave surged over.

"Hang on!" shouted Fergosi, his warning drowned out completely by the screams of the two others. An overpowering surge of water poured over them, wresting the couple's grips from their bench. Fergosi hit full speed as he tried to whip the bow toward the next surging whitecap. The boat was sluggish with the added weight of water, the fuel gauge was practically on empty, and Fergosi was desperate.

Margot lunged for the cabin, where she ducked down and started the boat's battery-powered bilge pumps with her shaking hands, but not before smashing her pate against the overhead. Brad barely managed to open a plug at the stern to allow the seawater to be pumped out.

Another swell slammed against the boat, but Fergosi turned the bow to a perfect angle, and *Motion of the Ocean* rode the wave's crest, where the ferry loomed only 500 yards away. Fergosi also noted with great relief that Block Island itself began offering some shelter from the surging storm swells. The sea suddenly grew calmer. Whitecaps still slapped over the boat, but the swells were several feet less in height. Thunder boomed above the roar of crashing waves.

Fergosi suspected that the ferry was only minutes away from entering the minefield. "Brad," he shouted. "Come here!"

"No way!" Brad moaned, clutching the bench for his life as he trembled from both cold and fear.

"Margot!" Fergosi tried.

She made her way to the driver's seat, clutching any hand hold she could find to keep herself from flying off the boat. She suddenly pointed and screamed, "In the water, dead ahead!"

Fergosi saw it tottering at the crest of a wave, the rusted metallic sphere of a sea mine, bristling with antenna-like detonators. He knew it was too late but made the valiant maneuver, anyway. *Motion of the Ocean*'s bow bit into the sea as it changed course, the boat leaning heavily from the force of the turn.

With a tremendous crash, the intrepid boat slammed into the mine. It was a glancing blow, but enough to break off two of the detonators. Fergosi shut his eyes as he waited for the loudest sound he would ever hear in his life, to be followed by what he assumed would be blackness, displaced by a tunnel of light with angels, deceased relatives, the sounds of bells and whatever else death brought.

What he heard was the familiar slap of another wave against the bow of the boat. *Motion of the Ocean* left the mine with its two broken detonators bobbing wildly in its wake. The thing was a dud!

Margot pointed and screamed, again.

* * * *

Frank Slade didn't believe in miracles, because he didn't believe in God. What he saw unfolding before him was one of those unpredictable quirks of nature, especially during a storm at sea. Usually, the surprises are bad, but not this time.

This is pure luck, Slade thought as he watched the horizon suddenly appear through his wind-and-salt-tortured eyes. Just like that, one second, nothing but whitecaps, spray and haze. Then, the storm suddenly lifted all the way to the horizon! In a few more seconds, the horizon became sharply defined, and the sea actually appeared calmer ahead of him. The swells decreased in size. He gunned the engine and plowed toward this badly needed respite.

Slade scanned the sea and saw Fergosi's craft disappearing behind a swell before him.

I've got you, you son of a bitch!

Fergosi's boat reappeared in the calmer water. Then it rose up...up...and it suddenly was sitting high on the horizon. Then, it vanished behind the...horizon?

What the hell...

A thin, white line appeared where *Motion of the Ocean* had disappeared. Then, other white lines began appearing at several places along the horizon. Then, the white lines grew thicker and started joining up, and in some places, they began spilling over as though in slow-motion. Then, the madman with the neck brace realized it wasn't the horizon. The term "wall of water" took on a new meaning as Slade watched the towering crests of the rogue wave finally come crashing down completely, the illusion of slow-motion caused by the enormity of the thing.

The roiling wall of white water surged toward him as fast as he was heading toward it. Slade's tormented mind saw no way to dodge this thing, nor did he have time to turn around and outrun it. It had him dead to rights. In one last act of defiance, the former football coach, driving instructor, and total failure gunned the engine and raced toward one of nature's most destructive forces. Had he been a World War II Japanese sailor, he might have been screaming "Banzai!" Instead, he just plain old screamed.

Holy Mackerel VI slammed into the wall, catapulting the shrieking Slade through the windscreen and into the air at a sixty-degree angle, while his hijacked boat flipped backward bow-over stern, disappearing into the whitewater meatgrinder below. His trajectory carried him higher and higher into the sky, bellowing rage and defiance the entire way.

* * * *

It was an entity unto itself. Smaller swells rippled across the width of the behemoth, and even they had their own chop, knocking *Shot Baker* to and fro as it rose higher and higher up the face of the rogue wave. Arnie gunned the engine to get his struggling craft to the wave's peak before it crested. When the powerful boat reached the summit, Brickley and his companions suddenly had a 360-degree view of the raging sea. He felt perched on a long, knife-edged mountain thrusting into the open sky. Yet, this mountain ridge was in constant motion. The smaller waves rippled to its crest, only to be atomized into pennants of spray by the shotgun wind.

In an instant, *Shot Baker* was slipping down the behemoth's backside in a slow fall, stomachs left high above. They all cried out with a unique sound—a combination of "Whoa!" and "Ahh!" as they became virtually weightless in the free-fall, their feet almost floating above the deck.

Arnie calmly surfed the craft down the slope and hit the trench-like trough at just the right angle to prevent *Shot Baker* from burying its bow or from capsizing. Suddenly, the wind stopped, and all was black. The dark swells surged upward all around them, as if they were in a hole in the ocean.

At this point, Brickley's bladder was unloading at a frightful rate.

They lurched to the top of another swell.

"Looks like we've got company!" shouted Arnie over the shriek of the wind and the engine's roar. Brickley followed Arnie's gaze and saw the heaving, yawing hull of another powerboat rise briefly above the frothy wave tops.

"That's gotta be Fergosi!" Brickley shouted, his sopping wet pants now sickly warm.

"You know who they are?" shouted Arnie.

"Yeah! My partner."

"Well, the more the merrier," Dora-Mae shouted. Then, "Oh, little Ikie's nervous and all wet. I'd better take him below."

* * * *

"Here!" Fergosi said, handing Margot the Beretta. "Always be sure that thing is pointed away from anything you don't want to shoot—always! And *never* have your finger touching that trigger except when you want to pull it. Okay? Keep an eye out for anything else in the water. If you see any sharks, shoot without hesitation! But don't shoot the boat!"

Margot held the gun as though it was a rabid skunk, while Brad watched Fergosi slide a magazine into his own 45, groaning as he realized that the cop's gun had been unloaded the entire time.

A Little Night Fishing

Sheltered from the rogue wave by Block Island, the ferry now wallowed through relatively calmer waters. *Motion of the Ocean* was now close enough to the ferry to see passengers staring at them from the windows. They pointed and gawked at the approaching powerboat being tossed like a toy in the waves.

Fergosi turned the boat parallel with the ship, decelerated, and scoured the water for mines. He aimed his 45 across the ferry's bow and fired.

Aboard the vessel, one passenger shrieked, "My God. He's shooting at us!"

Crew and passengers alike went from staring in shock to screaming and scrambling for cover as Fergosi fired another round. The ship plowed on, and nobody saw the mine directly in its path. *Motion of the Ocean* bored in, and Fergosi fired another round, then another.

"Stop, you fucking idiots!" Fergosi screamed. Margot and Brad stared at the whole scene in disbelief.

Fergosi noticed the bridge crew pointing at him and darting about like agitated ants. Through windows and portholes, the braver and un-seasick passengers gawked at the gun-toting lunatic aboard the cabin cruiser, while the others desperately pressed themselves face-first into the deck. Some pulled out their cell phones—finally.

Fergosi held up his badge in a futile effort to identify himself, then emptied his entire magazine in front of the ship's bow. The final round struck the mine, and it exploded in a towering pillar.

The water soared eighty feet, then hung motionless. Without warning, a shaft of lightning jabbed from the dark clouds to strike it, the crash of thunder coming right on the heels of the explosion. The blast sent a shock wave through the air that knocked Fergosi and Margot to the deck and sent Brad flying overboard. The cop gasped in awe, then stared blankly at his weapon.

* * * *

"There's the dinner bell," cried Otto to its comrades, which like dolphins, held themselves high out of the water by standing on their undulating tails to avoid the underwater shock of the explosion. "Let's go, folks, and remember to bring your appetites!" The whole pack slithered toward the ferry.

Otto was surprised when it didn't hear the screeches and squeals of a metal hull breaking up. A blast like that should have sent that chintzy bucket to the bottom in minutes. Then, it heard something that intrigued it even more. Other propellers had just entered open water from mainland waters and were heading this way.

* * * *

"I got it! So help me God, I got it!" Swynecock screamed triumphantly as he lowered the camera after the steaming geyser settled back into the water. "Grebe, my man, this is it! Get closer to that ferry. We're going to film a sinking ship!"

* * * *

"Brad!" Margot screamed. "Brad's overboard!"

Fergosi swung *Motion of the Ocean* around as Brad thrashed frantically upwind. Luckily for him, a swell caught him, slammed him against the side, and Fergosi and Margot were able to haul him back on board. Unluckily, blood from his injured nose was in the water.

* * * *

"Oh, my God. It hit a mine!" screamed Brickley as the fountain of water surged upward from the ferry's bow, only to be zapped by lightning. The roar and shock wave from the blast punched their ears and chests seconds later, followed by the thunderclap.

"Well, looks like you were right, Bob! This place is definitely mined!" shouted Dora-Mae from the cabin hatch.

"I told you we shouldn't have brought Ike along," snapped Arnie.

"I'll get in the bow and stand watch," said Dora-Mae, ignoring his remark.

The fortunate ferry had come to a complete halt. Al Fergosi realized that he had just taken the luckiest shot of his life. It was even luckier for the ferry's passengers and crew because, had Fergosi's shot not detonated the mine before the ship struck it head-on, they would have had only minutes, maybe seconds, to escape, and into turbulent seas at that.

Nevertheless, the force of the explosion burst several welds in the ferry's hull, and its bow began to settle slightly as water surged through the openings. Now, they had about fifteen minutes to escape. The captain and crew scrambled to prepare lifeboats, and the passengers stampeded for life vests. The wind and swells turned the ferry sideways, and it drifted at two knots away from Block Island and toward another mine.

* * * *

"This is when the sharks will start showing up," shouted Brickley, adrenaline surging through his body. "We have to get ready to pick up passengers!"

"Strictly speaking, we're over capacity now, with six people. These boats are all engine, and the cabin is small," called Arnie. "But we'll take on as many as we can."

He maneuvered *Shot Baker* forward, pulling as close as he dared to the sinking ferry. Then, he picked up a microphone next to the wheel and threw a switch. His voice boomed out over the wind and waves "*Island Lady, Shot Baker*. We are standing by off your port side to take on survivors if needed. Over."

Passengers were scurrying to the lifeboats as the ferry's deck continued to tilt forward. Then, a voice boomed from the ferry's bridge. "*Shot Baker, Island Lady*. Understood and thanks. We are loading lifeboats, but status unclear at this time. Please stand by. Over."

"*Island Lady, Shot Baker*. Will do. Out."

Arnie replaced the mike and looked around at his gun-toting passengers. "We should each take a practice shot just to be sure our weapons are functional. But that would create panic aboard the ferry, so we won't even think about it."

He saw that Shipley was looking extremely ill-at-ease with the shotgun. "Never fired one before?" he called over.

Shipley shook her head.

"Ever piloted a cigarette boat like this?" he asked.

"Yes, a few times," Shipley called back.

"Let's switch places, then. Why don't you give your shotgun to Mister Guard over there," he nodded to Brickley.

Shipley handed Brickley the shotgun, unclipped herself from the tether, and gratefully slid behind the wheel. Grasping his M-14, Arnie snapped in a magazine, then hooked himself into Shipley's tether.

"I don't mean to be a pain, but where are the terrorists we're supposed to shoot at?" Hulk shouted.

"They'll come out of the water," Brickley replied.

"Really?" asked Shipley. "Like Navy SEALs?"

"Like no SEALs you ever saw," Brickley responded. He then shoved two shells of heavy buckshot into the shotgun, and wondered despairingly whether he and his intrepid friends were going to find themselves on today's menu.

What the hell has happened to Fergosi?

"I think it's easier to shoot from a sitting position," offered Dora-Mae. "Eh, Army?" she looked at Hulk.

"That's absolutely right, ma'am!" he answered.

* * * *

Aboard the tilting, sinking ferry, the few who had remained calm were finally driven to panic by the flying rumor that the explosion had been the work of terrorists in the black boat. Only when they heard the booming exchange between Arnie and the ferry captain did the stampede for the lifeboats ease. The deck of the ferry tilted more and more. Two passengers—one tall and one short—wearing camouflaged caps tied securely under their chins, worked their way through the crowd and headed down to the lower deck.

"Women and children first!" the captain boomed over the public-address system.

"That's how they did it on the *Titanic*! This is just a stupid ferry boat," shouted a college kid of about twenty, wearing a shirt emblazoned with: World Peace, Boulder Colorado. "The captain is a sexist! I'll be damned if I'm going down in this trap just because I'm not a woman!"

He shoved a mother and her two crying children aside and bolted for the already overcrowded lifeboat that was swinging, more loosely than it should have been, from its davits. Suddenly, the captain's fist slammed into the space between "World" and "Peace", sending the student flying. The crowd backed away as the kid stumbled backward, only to hit the steel deck and slide forward to the superstructure.

The kid was quickly on his feet again, rubbing his head and enraged. "I'll fuckin' kill you!" he screamed, running blindly at the captain, only to crumple back to the deck from a solid punch to the cheekbone.

"Lower the boat!" ordered the captain, rubbing his knuckles. By the time the first lifeboat reached the waves, the bow of the ferry was disappearing, the stern had just lifted above the waterline, revealing its single screw, and the deck was tilting more and more. The heavy bow acted like the tip of a weather vane, pointing windward as the stern of the ship gently swung downwind, and only a few feet from the anchored mine.

In the automobile-packed hold, the men with the camouflaged hats leaped atop the hood of the first car and pranced and dented their way from hood to hood toward the rear, where their heavily loaded pickup truck tottered. The truck had U.S. Government plates. The tall one smashed the rear window of the truck, thrust his upper body through, pulled out a Mini-14 and handed it to his friend, along with a thirty-round magazine. Then, he extracted three Ingram MAC-10 machine pistols.

* * * *

"Okay, slow down, Grebe," a soaked Swynecock called gleefully as he filmed the sinking ship through a very wet camera. It was the last thing he ever said.

Fair & Square ran *directly* into a seaweed-covered mine with two broken detonators. Then boat and mine disintegrated in a massive explosion. Grebe was marinated, but before vanishing, he managed to absorb some of the shock of the explosion, prolonging the life of Flash Swynecock.

The hapless photographer catapulted sixty feet into the air, but he was somehow still conscious as he reached the perihelion of his unplanned flight. He bled profusely from the abundant folds of skin comprising his neck, thanks to the sudden arrival of his former understudy's jawbone, which tore into his neck like shrapnel, giving Swynecock the ultimate double chin. He saw below him the whitecap-shrouded sea, and directly below him, he saw the strangest sight of his life. To his dazed brain, it looked like a great white shark standing high out of the water, dancing on its tail just like Flipper.

It was clearly tracking him like an outfielder backpedaling

under a fly ball. Its maw was gaping, and Flash realized that the thing intended to catch him.

"You got 'im, leader! You got 'im!" croaked one of the renegade Karkarians as it watched Otto tracking the flying human. Its judgment of the airborne man's trajectory was right on the mark. Flash Swynecock never hit the water. He plunged right into Otto's waiting jaws, instead. Swynecock's squirming pelvis and legs dangled from Otto's teeth as it dashed wildly to its cheering section, slobbering.

"Tug o' war, dude!"

* * * *

The explosion snapped every head toward its sharp roar. People aboard the rapidly sinking ferry and the two lifeboats that had so far managed to get away began screaming, again.

Jaws dropped aboard *Shot Baker*, too.

"Oh, God! I hope that wasn't Fergosi's boat!" Brickley shouted, but his attention was arrested by something in the water not far from the blast zone. "There, in the water!" he screamed. "I see one! It's moving toward the ferry!"

Without thinking, he aimed and fired both barrels. The shot was high and to the right, striking the steel hull of the ferry, sending lead pellets ricocheting in every direction, and bringing another chorus of shrieks from the ferry passengers. The recoil sent Brickley sprawling backward.

"No!" cried Arnie. "You don't aim a shotgun! And that guy in the water is too far away. I thought you knew what the hell you..." Suddenly Arnie's gaze went back to "that guy in the water".

"What in God's name is that?" he called.

Whatever it was, it was coming closer, and more of them were heading toward the doomed ferry.

Brickley had already reloaded. He was ready when a shark-like head poked up about ten yards to port. He fired, again. The shark let loose a very non-shark yelp and grabbed the side of its head with what looked a great deal like hands. It stole a stunned look toward the wallowing cigarette boat, then disappeared beneath the surface.

"Jesus Christ! I don't believe this!" cried Wolf, pointing toward the steadily rising waterline of the ferry. The other five saw it, too. It was a head more human than shark, popping up and looking around.

"He's looking for people in the water," Brickley hollered.

"Aim low!" cried Dora-Mae.

A salvo of semiautomatic rifle fire blasted from *Shot Baker*, and the sea erupted with fountains of spray, blasting some ten feet into the air all around the predator. Suddenly, shots cracked from a different direction. The man-shark spun around to see a large human in another boat pointing a pistol at him. That was when a high-powered round fired from the sinking ship smashed into the shark's head, missed all vitals, and passed easily through the cartilage. An eruption of automatic fire then came from the two camo-capped passengers. Their high-velocity rounds slammed into the water in withering salvos, striking the shark several more times.

"We fight back in this country, you piece of shit!" screamed the taller guy, actually FBI agent Salvatore Cressi, part of a government team who had advance information about the attack.

Stunned but still alive, the predator-turned-prey quickly ducked below the sea's boiling surface and fled for its life, trailing blood and hoping that its "comrades" wouldn't follow.

The ferry's bow and its forward portholes slipped gradually but inexorably beneath the roiling surface. A third lifeboat lowered with great difficulty when the bedraggled college student suddenly jumped off the deck and into the lifeboat, landing on a woman and several children. The boat lurched to its side, dumping everyone into the heavy swells. All were wearing life vests and all heads popped to the surface, including the student's. He clawed onto a little girl bobbing in the water next to him, forcing her under.

Beneath the forest of kicking legs, Otto quickly forgot its concern about the gunfire. It greedily rubbed its hands together and wondered where to begin. It sized up the two humans gyrating more wildly than the others.

Sure enough, it thought. *One of the humans has panicked and is climbing all over a little one. What a moron! I'll start with him.*

The child, her lungs exploding, was seconds away from sucking seawater when the crazed student gave a quick yelp, and then disappeared. The little girl immediately popped back to the surface, gratefully sucking in air, while below her, an event was taking place that, if witnessed, would have driven her insane.

Otto pulled the student twenty feet under, life jacket and all, then bit off his feet and quickly bit into his calves before his life vest sent him upward. Then, with crazed thrusts of its jaw, began swallowing him. Its powerful throat gripped him, and with tremendous spasms, began forcing the dying student deeper into its gullet. His upper body, face frozen amid a mind-wrenching scream, protruded from the Karkarian's mauling teeth, his blood beginning to cloud the water. Bubbles still issued from the dead mouth—a tremendous turn-on for his killer. Otto's entire body was now heaving with the contractions that forced the corpse deeper and deeper, until only the victim's head remained exposed.

* * * *

The wind continued to push the ferry away from Block Island, and the stern was only seconds from brushing against the rusty mine. Despite the increasing angle of the deck, more gunfire erupted from the ferry.

In the hold, twenty-five cars and trucks also tilted crazily. Then, it happened. In the last row of vehicles, an SUV slipped forward and bumped the car ahead of it. Both then skidded into the row of cars in front, and this touched off a screeching avalanche. The tremendous shift in weight caused the ship's bow to dip another ten feet in just a few seconds, kicking the angle of the deck to fifty degrees. Passengers started screaming, again. Those not holding onto something that was part of the ship immediately lost their footing, and a landslide of life-vest-clad bodies, fire extinguishers, trash bins, and luggage tumbled down the decks to crash into the sea.

* * * *

Three Karkarians were gathered on the sea bottom nearby. They heard and felt the ferry's death throes, as well as Otto gulping down a passenger not far away.

"I've been shot!" whined one. Its face had three shotgun pellets buried deeply. Fortunately for it, the bleeding was minimal.

"This isn't working out the way the leader said it would," clicked another. They turned upward at the muffled sound of yet more gunfire. "I mean, they're not supposed to defend themselves! Where the hell are all these guns coming from?"

"And listen. There are more powerboats coming! I say we get outta here!"

It was then that the blood from the wounded "comrade" began filtering into the senses of the other two. Their nostrils and faces began to twitch, and their eyes grew wild.

"No!" squeaked the wounded one, but it was too late. In seconds, the others fell upon it, ripping its flesh and biting huge chunks of meat from its flailing body.

* * * *

The ferry's propeller reared higher and higher. The groaning, creaking ship was now sliding downward twice as quickly as it had been. There were only minutes left, and on deck, it was "every man for himself". Except for the FBI team, who stopped hunting for Karkarian targets long enough to find something to brace themselves against.

Just as the last passengers jumped into the water, the keel of the ferry finally bumped into the mine. The blast sent a geyser of water 100 feet into the air and flipped the stern up and over the bow. While the stricken hull protected many of those in the water from the shock wave of the immense explosion, the flipping vessel killed many others as its topside slammed into the water, again. A bolt of lightning struck the bronze screw with a crash of thunder that made many victims believe that Judgment Day was upon them.

Island Lady rolled lazily onto her port side, but not before the two FBI men managed to pick off two more Karkarians, sling their weapons, and jump. Then, the vessel capsized and, with bubbles the size of SUVs bursting violently around the hull, she finally sank beneath the waves.

On the sea floor 120-feet below, among the scraps of shark meat and blood, two Karkarians writhed and quivered as every organ in their bodies ruptured from the titanic blast of the mine, their suffering cut short by the hulk of the descending ferry wreck.

Near the surface, Otto and its mate thought they were done for. The shock wave from the explosion stunned them into delirium, knocking out their sonar, numbing their lateral lines, and jolting their brains. Just having cartilage to guard their brains instead of good, solid bone didn't do much to cushion the blast. Otto couldn't tell which direction was up, and it just lolled around at the surface for more than a minute.

Then, a wave of nausea overtook it, and in one prodigious heave, what was left of the student and Flash Swynecock ejected from its maw. Somewhat sheltered from the shock wave by Otto's massive body, the mate hadn't been dazed enough to lose its appetite. It first nibbled, and then devoured, Otto's discharge.

"That's my girl," Otto mumbled affectionately, already feeling better.

It tried to shake the ringing from its head, realizing only then that the ringing was, in fact, the sound of approaching powerboats. Otto popped to the surface, peering across the seascape dotted with boats, swells, and helpless people bobbing in orange life vests.

* * * *

"Survivor in the water," shouted a Coast Guardsman from the deck of a powerful, forty-seven-foot motor lifeboat. The sailor had just spotted the struggling figure, mostly obscured by the rafts of brownish foam and white-capped swells. The coxswain maneuvered the vessel, and the crew jumped to their well-rehearsed rescue procedures. They scooped up the man whose neck brace-turned-flotation-device had kept his head above the water and thus saved his life.

* * * *

"That's it. We're outta gas," shouted Fergosi as the engine coughed, then fell silent. He'd just steered *Motion of the Ocean* to the edge of the sea of struggling people who flailed on the surface amid the debris and air bubbles boiling over the ferry's grave.

"There are plenty of people alive, and now, we can't go in and get 'em!" Then, he cupped his hands to his mouth. "Anybody who can swim for us, we'll take you aboard!"

The nearest survivors heard Fergosi and started to swim toward his voice. He could see other boats riding up and down in the heaving swells. Just then, two Coast Guard HH-65C Dolphin helicopters roared overhead, but the whole scene of wreckage was drifting away from the shelter of Block Island

and back into the worst of the storm. The sky darkened even more, and the wind gusted to sixty miles per hour, blowing Fergosi's helpless craft away from the survivors.

The cop cursed loudly and stomped his feet in helpless rage. Fergosi suddenly took heart as he spotted a Coast Guard "47" headed his way, the familiar white hull and blue/red "racing stripe" boosting his spirit.

"Thank God!" Fergosi shouted and, for the first time on this crazy trip, Margo and Brad smiled, too.

Fergosi jumped up and down, waving to the rescue vessel. "Over here!" he sang, upon which the "47" disintegrated in a shattering blast whose shock wave knocked Fergosi to the deck.

Once again, the dazed driving instructor found himself hurtling through the air, this time at a much higher velocity and leading a tower of water, smoke, debris, and sailors, most of them unconscious or dead. Fergosi stared in shock as pieces of the patrol boat and its hapless crew arched downward and began splashing into the ocean. Two more Coast Guard boats came to a complete halt, and the helicopters roared back to the scene. Two television news choppers were now orbiting the scene, obviously having trouble keeping stable in the wind.

Suddenly, Fergosi caught the incongruous sound of clapping and a rumbly kind of laughing over the wind and waves. He turned and spotted five not-so-human heads bobbing over the swells only about fifty yards away.

"Wa-hoo!" one called, clapping its hands over its head. "Encore!

"There!" Fergosi shrieked with rage, pointing him out to the Brad and Margot. "There's a bunch of 'em!"

"A bunch of what? What are those?" Margot squeaked.

"Let 'em have it!" Fergosi snapped off five quick shots.

Margot fired three times from the bucking deck as Brad groaned, the blood from his nose injury now drying on his face.

One of Margot's shots struck the water, nowhere close to the monsters. Apparently having no taste for a fight against firearms, all the Karkarians except one retreated beneath the waves. Margot's next two shots punched holes through the gunwale of their own boat. Then, she fell to her hands and knees, vomiting. At the same moment, Brad tried to get to his feet to help her, only to have a high swell tilt the deck and dump him overboard again with a heartrending cry.

* * * *

"Otto's head spun toward the sound of the gunfire, only to see fountains kicked up by shots from a different direction. It spun its head again, only to see the large, black cigarette boat, with its raked bow, streaking toward him, two wet-suit clad people peeling off shot after shot.

Otto ducked beneath the waves. Its rage tore it maddeningly between pursuing its cowardly companions and tearing to bits these humans who had the incredible arrogance to ruin its plans for a feast.

* * * *

"We gotta' get to the survivors and pull in as many as we can, injured people first," Arnie shouted to Shipley at *Shot Baker*'s helm.

A sixty-five mile-per-hour gust ripped across the water, bringing with it a blinding wall of rain as Patti Shipley skillfully swung the bow of the cigarette boat toward the sea of bobbing, crying people. Hulk and Wolf threw extra life vests among them.

"Get us out! There are sharks!" a woman screamed.

"Over there!" called Dora-Mae, pointing to starboard. Shipley glided alongside a mother and two small, sobbing children. Brickley, Hulk, and Arnie began hauling them aboard while Wolf tottered on the deck, the M14 pressed tightly against her shoulder as she scanned the sea for predators.

* * * *

As the helicopters and rescue swimmers plucked people from the water, the two remaining Coast Guard "47s", well separated from each other but not equipped with sonar, cautiously picked their way through the bucking seas toward the forty or so people remaining in the water. The survivors were quickly becoming divided in the rough seas and pummeling rain.

* * * *

Among the flotsam was a neck brace.

In fact, the turbulence from the explosion in such deep water had caused a brief, spinning, tornado-like vortex that sucked the surface water almost to the sea bottom, pulling nearly everything down with it. That included Frank Slade who, incredibly, had sustained relatively minor injuries in the two blasts. Now, still conscious, he was being dragged to the bottom. The former coach's eardrums had already burst from the pressure at eighty feet, but when the underwater tornado spat him out on the sea floor at 120 feet, the pressure of the relatively undisturbed water was far greater. This compressed the luckless man's body, forcing seawater into every orifice, including his tear ducts. Combined with the shock waves from the explosions, and the trauma of crashing through the *Holy Mackerel VI*'s windscreen, the pressure triggered something.

It triggered something despite this torture, because Frank Slade wasn't dead. That's because he was different. He carried The Gene.

The Karkarians could, and would, explain it all to him. It was an eon-old mutation that only a few humans carried with them, and most of those carried it, unsuspected, to the grave. In those few who endured the right aquatic circumstances, The Gene caused a change, not unlike what occurs in the pine cones of the giant sequoia, which need the intense, thousand-degree heat of a massive forest fire to release their seeds.

Slade's outer body literally peeled off. The intense pressure flattened his arms and legs, and the bones changed. In a few more minutes, they looked like nothing so much as fins. Folds of skin on his neck transmuted into gills. Soon, its head elongated, sharpened, and became shark-like.

As if nature was replacing her losses, another Karkarian entered the world. What had been Frank Slade sped off into the depths of its new home, with stomach empty and still very pissed off.

* * * *

Fergosi was on the radio. "Coast Guard, *Motion of the Ocean*. This is Sergeant Alphonse Fergosi of the Easterly, Rhode Island, Police. Do you copy? There are sharks in the water going after survivors. Also, I am without power and drifting. Do you copy? Over."

"*Motion of the Ocean*, Coast Guard helo 6529. Copy that, sir. Can you identify other vessels in vicinity of sinking? Over."

"Coast Guard 6529, *Motion of the Ocean*. Also police and apparently, some civilians. They are guarding survivors and effecting rescues." Through the increasing rain, Fergosi could barely see the helicopter hovering in the distance.

"Roger that." There was a pause, then, "Are you aware full situation: hostiles in the water?"

Fergosi was stunned. Was it possible that the Coast Guard knew about these monsters, too?

"That's affirmative, 6529. Are you?"

"*Motion of the Ocean*, Coast Guard 6529. Roger that. Be advised that an FBI team was aboard *Island Lady*. Need to recover them if possible. Additional Coast Guard and National Guard units on the wa..."

Fergosi could see it only dimly, but the helicopter's white tail flew violently upward, flipping the aircraft amid the column of water from yet another massive blast. There was no other debris. Fergosi realized that the sheer turbulence of the ocean must have set off another mine.

"No!" he screamed as pieces of the aircraft hung motionless for a moment, then flew off into the wind. He fell to the deck and painfully dry-heaved as *Motion of the Ocean* drifted helplessly from the scene.

* * * *

Not far away, *Shot Baker* was purring alongside a huddled group of five survivors.

"Anybody hurt?" Dora-Mae called.

"Yes! Help," they shouted. Then, two of them screamed and shot below the surface.

Pulling the screaming tourists 100 feet to the bottom, Otto and its mate forced them down their gullets. "Yumm!" it gurgled and patted its bulging, writhing stomach. It turned to look at what had once been a woman, herself a shipwreck victim in a life long past and half-forgotten. "Her" last victim's legs still protruded grotesquely from its mouth.

"Otto looked back up at the maze of legs and the sleek keel of the cigarette boat among them.

The hulk of the ferry lay on its side on the sandy floor of Block Island sound. Air bubbles and oil leaked upward. A lifeboat, attached to its mooring only by the bow line, floated like a kite above the ship. From behind the boat, the "enforcer"—known to its own clan as the *electis*—watched Otto and its mate devour their meals. The next thing it saw them do sickened even it. Like the lovers they were, each took turns sticking their tail fins down each other's throats, complete with affectionate grunts and clicks, as they regurgitated their horrible loads to make room for more.

* * * *

There was only one approaching Coast Guard boat left, and that one wasn't going anywhere near the minefield, which took the pressure off Otto and its mate. They reasoned that they had at most a half hour before some serious guns arrived. It was time to "take a hike" and look for "greener" waters down the coast. The mate wanted to rest before the next course, while Otto and its freshly emptied stomach were in the mood for more.

"I'll be right back, lover," it grunted. "We've only got time for a couple more humans."

As Otto swam to the surface, the figure of a twelve-foot humanoid shark eased from behind the lifeboat, moved to the bottom, then crept toward Otto's mate. It felt "Bob" approaching and turned to see it materialize from the murk, holding a gleaming spear gun in one hand.

"Hello, sweetie," it burbled.

* * * *

The throb of a large, low-flying plane filled the air and penetrated the water. A white C-130 with the Coast Guard "racing stripe" blazing on its fuselage swooped below the rain squall to drop dozens of rubber lifeboats and life preservers among the now-scattered survivors. Mixing with the roar of its engines and the rumble of thunder was the *thump-thump* of approaching Marine Corps Super Cobra attack helicopters.

* * * *

"Honey, I'm home!" clicked Otto cheerfully as it returned

to the bottom holding two more thrashing, dying, life-vested victims by their feet.

There was no answer.

It called, again. Then, its nostril picked up a vague scent of blood—his mate's blood. Otto released the two humans, whose bodies went rocketing back to the surface. It tried to follow the trail of blood but didn't get far before losing it. This was the first time in its second life that Otto had lost a trail of blood.

"Are you all right?" it squealed loudly. The only sounds it heard were air bubbles still escaping from the wreck, the sloshing turbulence on the surface, the whine of an idling Coast Guard boat, and buzz from the propeller of another. It thought of the cabin cruiser that had turned off its engine.

Wait a minute. Turned off its engine? In these seas? I don't think so. That boat's disabled!

Just thinking the word "disabled" made Otto's predatory instinct surge through him like a rush of adrenaline.

"Disabled" means helpless! God, that word drives me wild!

It lost interest in its mate and followed the drive of instinct.

Chapter Fourteen

The rain and thunder eased. It seemed that Hurricane Avril had turned west and was going to make landfall in New Jersey, some 200 miles down the coast.

The lumbering C-130 swooped low again, seemingly frustrated that it couldn't land in the water to rescue survivors, and several more rubber rafts tumbled wildly from its cargo door. More Coast Guard vessels, along with police boats from every nearby port, were on the way. The *thump-thump* of the Marine helos grew ever louder.

Motion of the Ocean wallowed helplessly in the still-formidable waves as its remaining occupants lay incapacitated by nausea in the foul mixture of seawater, rainwater, and vomit. Al Fergosi, his .45 jammed into his belt, forced himself up from his hands and knees, and he staggered to the pilot's chair. Another wave jolted the boat, and Fergosi reeled over, landing heavily against the deck. He picked himself up slowly and, as he reached for the radio, the boat tipped, again. Somehow, this shock felt distinctly different from what a wave would do.

Fergosi looked up just in time to see the hideous, human-shark figure of Otto heaving itself onto the boat, to loom, dripping, above him with a wild leer on its face. The cop knew immediately that this wasn't the Karkarian he'd met on West Beach.

Fergosi reached for his weapon, but Otto was faster, slapping the .45 from Fergosi's hand and sending it overboard.

"Careful, big guy," mocked "Otto." "You'll hurt yourself with a nasty thing like that. Me? I used to be a U-boat officer. I know how to handle guns, mines, and shit like that." Then, he spotted the Beretta lying half-submerged on the deck.

"Another one? No fair!" it rumbled as it tossed that weapon overboard. "I mean, two against one is bad enough, but you need two guns as well? Kinda cowardly, if you ask me."

Fergosi tried to get a grip on reality as this perfect predator stood steadily on the heaving deck. As a police sergeant, he wasn't accustomed to being insulted. Being called a coward by some monster out of a horror movie pierced right through his consuming seasickness.

Otto's contemptuous gaze shifted from Fergosi to Margot, who gaped in frozen terror.

"Which one shall I taste first?" it burbled.

Fergosi guessed that the creature had a good ten-inch reach on him, and to fight one that big, the only strategy was to stay in close. He struggled to his feet and stepped toward Otto, who read his intentions exactly. Fergosi's fist swung drunkenly at Otto's stomach, but the monster easily leaned back, out of the way. Lightning-fast, the creature then leaned down and slammed its huge fist into Fergosi's already tortured stomach. The man crumpled to the deck.

* * * *

Shot Baker was already overflowing with survivors, most seasick and all in shock. Bob Brickley spotted *Motion of the Ocean* drifting in the distance. He asked Arnie for his binoculars, and what Brickley saw brought him to the brink of panic. He saw Otto battering Al Fergosi with his fists and feet, the man sprawling to the deck like a rag doll, only to be hauled to his feet and punched, again.

"We've gotta help my partner! A shark's on his boat and is kicking the shit out of him," Brickley yelled.

Shipley shouted, "Hang on!" as she swung the bow toward Fergosi's boat, then hit the throttle. Those standing fell to the deck as the cigarette boat lurched like a stallion across the waves in spite of its load.

"Mine dead ahead," shouted Dora-Mae, still on watch at the bow. Shipley slowed and eased the boat well clear of the menace, then accelerated straight for the disabled cabin cruiser. *Shot Baker* was soon close enough, less than a hundred yards away, for Brickley to watch in horror as Otto started to raise Fergosi's limp body like a bunch of grapes over its open mouth. Brickley pointed the shotgun, but Arnie voiced what Brickley already knew: The chances were equal that he'd hit Fergosi as well as the thing.

"Damn it!" cried Dora-Mae, her rifle at her shoulder. "I'm not sure enough of my aim in these seas!"

"Shoot, or he'll die anyway!" Brickley screamed as Fergosi's

A Little Night Fishing

head dangled above Otto's gaping maw.

Even as Dora-Mae started to squeeze the trigger, they all gaped as another towering shape heaved itself onto *Motion of the Ocean*. It was another shark-man, and Brickley recognized the object it was brandishing. Even at this distance he could see that it was his own lost spear gun!

Otto's head tilted upward and its eyes rolled backward into their protective eyelids. Its body wracked with spasms as its prodigious gullet began forcing down its substantial meal. Then, it sensed a large presence that hadn't been there a second before. The human was a quarter of the way down and proving to be a much tougher meal to swallow than Otto had ever experienced. It realized that it was completely vulnerable.

"Hello, 'Otto'," uttered the "enforcer" coolly as it raised the spear gun.

Otto tried desperately to haul Fergosi out of its gullet.

The warriors aboard *Shot Baker* gazed at the spectacle in abject horror. Brickley focused on the spear gun, his jaw dropping as he stared at the top-of-the-line, very expensive weapon clutched in the shark-man's hands. He saw that if the "enforcer" fired the spear, it would plunge through Otto and might hit Fergosi, too.

"Hey! 'Bob'!" Brickley screamed. "Aim low!"

Bob? thought the others, in spite of their terror.

With a *thunk*, the spear blasted into Otto's chest. Too high! Fergosi's legs jolted from the impact of the spear slamming through him. Otto's arms flapped wildly, but only for a second as the "enforcer" fell on him.

"Get Al out," Brickley frantically shouted, but the "enforcer," its body metamorphosing into its shark form, lunged open-mouthed at "Otto," biting into its neck and shaking it violently, knocking all three of them to the heaving deck.

Meanwhile, Shipley brought *Shot Baker* as close as she dared to the leeward side of *Motion of the Ocean*. Brickley leaped aboard and spotted a woman lying helplessly at the stern as he scrambled for the huge, humanoid-shark bodies struggling violently on the deck. Joya Wolf, Hulk Hoagland, and Patti Shipley leaped bravely aboard behind Brickley.

"Open his jaws! Get my friend out before he dies!" Brickley shrieked, but the "enforcer's" death grip remained locked as Otto's blood poured from its neck as well as from the spear that solidly impaled its body and its prey's.

Brickley foolishly tried to tear the "enforcer" off, first gripping its sandpaper dorsal fin, then grabbing its nose, but the man-shark was too strong. Fergosi's legs had stopped kicking. Brickley desperately started clubbing the "enforcer" with the butt of the shotgun, but to no avail.

All of a sudden, there was an explosion of automatic cannon fire not far away. The Marine helicopters were firing at something in the water. Brickley and the others paid no attention.

"Get me a gaff," shouted Brickley to Margot. She was too shocked and sick to respond. He tottered and staggered across the bucking deck to the compartments in the transom. Buried under a life vest and hand pump was a short-handled gaff.

About time I had some luck!

He jammed the hook of the gaff into Otto's lower jaw and yanked back with all his might, grunting and gasping from the effort. Slowly, the jaw yielded, its teeth lifting from Fergosi's bleeding wounds.

"Pull him out! I can't hold it open much longer!"

Shipley and Wolf each grabbed a foot and began tugging, then yanking. Arnie leaped aboard, grabbed a leg, and called, "One! Two! Three! Everybody pull!"

Fergosi wouldn't budge.

"The spear's pinning him! Pull out the spear!"

Wolf yanked at the spear, and Fergosi's feet twitched. The spear was lodged solidly.

"You've got to push the spear all the way through, fasten the barbs, and then pull it back," Brickley called.

"What?" cried Wolf. This was too much even for a tough gal.

"Push the spear through and clip the barbs into that little band thing. Now, before he's too far gone!" Brickley screamed.

"I don't get it!"

"Joya, grab the gaff!" Brickley gasped. "I'll deal with the spear!"

The "enforcer" was writhing as Otto's blood streamed from its now gaping wounds, covering the deck and making it even more slippery.

There was a sudden burst of automatic-weapons fire from a Coast Guard forty-five-foot Response Boat in the distance.

Fortunately, Otto was on his side, the spear parallel to the deck. Brickley grabbed the spear and, screaming with frantic, adrenaline-pumped energy, heaved it the rest of the way through Otto's bulk. The tip burst from the creature's back. Fergosi's feet twitched one last time.

Brickley leaped over the bodies, quickly fastened the twin barbs of the spear's tip into their holder, then vaulted back, grabbed the spear and yanked with a desperate, banshee screech, throwing his entire weight behind it. The spear pulled out with relative ease, sending Brickley flying backward. He then lunged at Fergosi's now limp feet and desperately pulled.

With one huge heave, Fergosi, covered with blood and slime, popped from Otto's jaws. Brickley and Wolf dragged him to the bow, well away from the still-struggling monsters. Blood oozed from Fergosi's left shoulder, where the spear had, miraculously, missed everything but muscle and bone.

If he's still alive, he needs mouth-to-mouth resuscitation, Brickley knew.

"Patti!" Brickley shrieked. He then scooped the shotgun from the deck.

A whitecap suddenly broke across Motion of the Ocean, its torrent washing the two Karkarians across the deck and against a gunwale. As Shipley, undaunted by the blood and slime, began mouth-to-mouth on Fergosi, Brickley cracked the gun, loaded two shells, then crawled across the bucking deck toward the "enforcer" and "Otto."

His body covered with brine and his mouth dry, Brickley stepped toward the battling giants. He hesitated, then stood and aimed. Just as he pulled both triggers, a wave slammed into the hull, knocking Brickley off his feet. The blast glanced off Otto's massive head, shocking the "enforcer" so much that it released its grip. The shot blew a hole in the deck.

"Otto," a ragged red wound revealing his cartilaginous skull, thrashed about on the deck as its eyes spun behind closed eyelids. Brickley stared in horror at the result of his bungled attempt. The grotesque demon pitched and squirmed as blood poured from the gaping gouge.

With crazed eyes, the dazed "enforcer" eased back and shook its head, completely deafened by the shotgun blast. Suddenly, to Brickley's horror, Otto struggled to its feet but faltered and began to sway backward. With shocking speed, the "enforcer" metamorphosed into a half-human again, rose to its feet, and lunged at its enemy, and the momentum of its attack sent them both plunging overboard.

Then, Brickley heard coughing and gagging behind him. Nonplussed, he turned to see Fergosi's body heaving as his lungs began working, again. Straddling him, Shipley looked like a proud mother.

"I can't believe he's alive!" she cried. "The spear didn't hit anything major, and the thing never bit down. God, it's a miracle!"

"Yeah, I think he's going to live," shouted Wolf, trying to keep her footing nearby.

Brickley staggered to the edge of the gunwale and stared overboard into the foaming, ink-black, and bloody sea where the two creatures disappeared.

I have a feeling...no, I'm certain that I'll never, ever see them again, he thought with a sense of relief.

Brickley allowed himself to rest. He had done his best.

Holmes never had a case like this!

As he knelt in the polluted, bilgy brine, catching his breath while shivering like a paint mixer, his gaze swept across the wild, surreal, and undulating seascape, and he began to feel a sense of closure to this nightmare. The helicopters were still hovering, but the firing had stopped. *Shot Baker* purred nearby, with an anxious-looking Arnie, Dora-Mae, and a collection of survivors peering toward them. A Coast Guard "47" wasn't far off, still rescuing people.

Brickley saw the sea in a way he never had, and hoped that he never would, again: An eye-level view of mountainous swells with spilling whitecaps that completely surrounded him. There was a sullen beauty. He turned and rested his elbows on the gunwale. The worst was over.

Thank God.

A grotesque hand burst from the blackness below and grabbed Brickley's collar. The half-shark, half-human face of the "enforcer" rose from the depths like the face of the devil and came nose-to-nose with Brickley.

"How many humans did you and the other one tell? Look at this!" it bellowed, motioning to the military aircraft and vessels. "You didn't keep your word, you traitor, and I'm going to kill you!"

Brickley was incredulous but, much to his own surprise, kept his wits. "What are you talking about? They already knew!"

"Thanks to you—you little prick!"

Brickley came right back at it. "Of course, you strolling into the Titanic Café stark naked and attacking the light fixtures didn't grab any attention!"

"You listen to me..."

"No, you listen to me, you jackass!" Brickley sputtered.

Behind him, Joya Wolf murmured "Redemption" and carefully picked up Brickley's long-lost spear gun, which was sliding around the deck in the bloody, foamy water.

"Like you standing totally naked on the rocks, shouting at me in front of my friends didn't open a few eyes?"

Brickley ripped his collar from the thing's grip and shot to his feet. He gestured with a sweeping arm at the surrounding calamity. "You did a great job preventing this massacre! I mean, you've done nothing, and I've done everything! You didn't give a shit about my friend, risking his life doing what you should have been doing—stopping your kind from doing all this!"

The "enforcer" was outraged. "'Otto' got away, you moron! I *had* him, then *you* shoot that fuckin' gun off—and don't kill him! Nothing's been accomplished! The whole thing's blown wide open, and it's *your* fault!"

There was an imperceptible *click* as Wolf slid the spear into firing position. Her skinny arms and delicate hands pulled the massive thrust bands back with hate-driven strength and clipped them into the spear. She released the safety.

"Redemption," she whispered.

"'Otto' got away?" Brickley gasped. "But he was almost dead!"

"You're the one who's going to be dead!"

At that moment, the "enforcer" caught sight of the petite figure rising smoothly from behind the gunwale and aiming the spear gun straight at his face. With lightning speed, he ducked before Wolf could loose.

Brickley fell back, his head landing hard against the bloody, wet deck. Everything moved in super-slow motion. Joya Wolf seemed surrounded by a hazy white and gold light that suddenly spread into a brilliant halo around her head. He looked closer and saw her face distorted with murderous rage.

All at once, *Motion of the Ocean* snapped to a forty-five-degree angle as a low, powerful breaker smashed into the port side, sending Brickley sliding across the deck. Wolf's bare feet were solidly splayed, ready to strike like the predator she was.

In a queasy, dazed dream, Brickley watched her leap for the gunwale and, as in so many nightmares, he struggled to shout but couldn't make a sound. She started to spring over the railing like a jaguar, and that was when Brickley realized that clutched in her hands was his treasured, yet so elusive, spear gun. He reached into the empty wind to stop her as a desperate scream finally burst from his very soul, *"No!"*

Chapter Fifteen

Three days later, the memorial service for the victims of the ferry "accident" was as any memorial service should be. People cried and said wonderful things about the deceased. Children sat stunned if they'd lost someone, or fidgeted if they hadn't.

Brickley still couldn't believe that Joya Wolf was gone, especially because there was no body. He couldn't shed a single tear. Patti Shipley bawled.

Brickley remembered seeing the memorial plaques to drowned seamen in other New England towns, like New Bedford and Gloucester. He recalled the beginning of *Moby Dick*, about people lost at sea, with part of the agony being the inability to actually witness that their husbands, fathers, or sons were actually dead…not knowing where in the sea their bodies rested.

Or whether they'd been caught by the Karkarians.

Because there might be more "rogue sharks", and more of those World War II mines floating around that had somehow escaped detection for almost seventy years in heavily traveled waters—it was too dangerous for recovery divers to search for Wolf's body, or those of the thirty-eight others who had lost their lives. At least, that's what the government said.

As he left the church by himself, Brickley's rage gnawed at him, because he knew where Wolf must be. Surely, she must be in the "enforcer's" digestive tract, or Otto's, if he'd really escaped. That finally brought home the fact that Joya Wolf was dead.

Maybe, I should cry after all, Brickley thought.

He tried to cheer himself with the recent news that the guy who'd fallen overboard from Fergosi's boat, Brad, had turned up delirious but alive, albeit in a slimy pile of squid on the deck of an intrepid fishing boat.

Like something out of a storybook.

What had gone on for the witnesses in the previous three days had been like something out of a book too, and not a

Sherlock Holmes story, either. More like a horror novel.

The FBI and other agents he couldn't identify had corralled him, Patti Shipley and Hulk Hoagland, along with Arnie and Dora-Mae, whose last name turned out to be Blackmon. They had been isolated in an old military building at Quonset Point, on Narragansett Bay, for a day and a half of questioning, threats to keep their mouths shut, and stupid explanations for what they'd seen. At the end, however, the guy who'd seemed to be in charge had hinted about a "project" Brickley might be called upon to help them with. Brickley strongly suspected that he might be of interest, because he had interacted with the Karkarians and lived to talk about it. Time would tell.

Over that day and a half, however, Brickley had found out one thing he wasn't supposed to know, or was he? Somebody had carelessly left the door to a laboratory unlocked. It was a room that he and the others weren't supposed to enter. Brickley entered, and on a table, he'd found and read a brief but very thorough report about The Gene.

Meanwhile, Fergosi was in a medically induced coma in a Boston hospital. He'd probably be there for a month, then most likely to rehab. Brickley planned to drive up to see him as soon as the dust settled in Tuckernut, if it ever did. At least, he had his summer job back. All people knew was that he and Patti Shipley had led one of the impromptu rescue boats and had saved many lives. He was a local hero, again.

Hurricane Avril had raised hell in New Jersey, and the New England coast was little the worse for wear, at least physically.

Still numb, Brickley wandered onto the boardwalk toward West Beach, realizing that he couldn't wait for this damned summer to be over, so he could go back to Tuckernut Elementary. He never thought he'd look forward to a room full of rowdy fourth graders, again.

Elementary School, my dear Watson.

Taking off his shoes and stepping onto West Beach was an intensely sensual affair. He felt the warm sand between his toes, and he greedily inhaled the virgin ocean air that had traveled untainted from so far across the vastness of the sea, now calm again. There's something about the ocean that makes you honest, and Brickley almost always felt his perspective clarify at times like this. The experience always made him realize that life and the universe were so much bigger than his little life and petty problems.

But not today. The grisly thought of Joya Wolf at the bottom of the sea—inside or outside a Karkarian—swam before Brickley's mind, again. The thought would haunt him forever, he knew. Would he be the one to discover her remains the next time he was diving? With what he'd been through, would there be a next time? Would he ever go in the water, again?

The FBI insisted that the military had wiped out the Karkarians.

How would that be possible? How many people—how many of us—have The Gene?

Even though Avril had gone elsewhere, her power eroded the beach by one-third. So, when Brickley came to the three fishermen's murder scene, he saw that it was under four feet of water. He kept walking. He was sick of it all.

Ahead of him, he was shocked to see the exhausted figure of a scuba diver sitting peacefully at the water's edge, seeming not to notice or care about the waves washing briskly over her legs and threatening to scoop into the sea her tanks, which were lying carelessly on the sand next to her.

What's this jerk doing scuba diving when there's still a shark warning?

Then, Brickley noticed that this person was watching him closely, a slight smile on her face. When he turned to meet her eyes, he was struck by lightning as she pulled off her diving hood. He froze and stared at her in the same way anyone would stare at a person who'd returned from the dead.

"Joya!" Brickley gasped.

"Hi, Bob Brickley," she responded distantly.

"My God! You're alive?"

"Yeah, and I'm supposed to tell you something."

Before she could say another word, Brickley burst into hysterical laughter and smothered her with an enormous hug, knocking them both flat just in time for a wave to wash over them.

As she lay on her back, covered with wet sand, Wolf's gaze continued to be happy but distant.

"Where did the scuba gear come from?" bubbled Brickley as they stood up.

"Oh, it was the 'enforcer'. You know him as 'Bob'. Whatever you call him, he gave it to me. He said he 'borrowed' it from a scuba diver he met not too long ago diving the sunken U-boat by Block Island."

"Oh, right! Very funny!" said Brickley through his gorilla grin. "But really...what happened? Where have you been the last three days? Everybody's been—"

"I have a message for you," Wolf repeated.

The look on her face told Brickley that this was no joke. His felt his blood chill.

"I'm supposed to tell you that he's willing to make a deal with you," she stated.

"Make a deal?"

"Yes, a deal. And here are the terms..."

Wolf told him, in detail.

Brickley stared blankly at the horizon. "Oh, shit," he finally murmured. Looking back at Wolf, he said, "Let me help you take this gear back to my car. I'll give you a lift to your car."

"I don't have my car."

"I'll take you home, then." Brickley was becoming frightened. He wasn't sure why.

"I'm not going back there," Wolf stated flatly.

"What?"

"I'm going to be staying," she said, staring out to sea with a distant smile. "This is my home."

Oh, God! It can't be! Brickley's mind reeled.

"I'm going back," Wolf said. "Into the sea. It's where we all came from in the first place, you know. But some of us don't stay away for long. Besides, I'm in love!"

"What..." Brickley blurted.

"I'm in love, Bob Brickley. This time, it's the real thing."

"Who?"

She looked Brickley directly in the eye for the first time. "'Bob', the 'enforcer', or whatever you want to call him!"

Brickley stared at her with golf ball eyes.

Wolf was amused. "Look, remember when I dove in after him? I took a shot at him and missed. He grabbed me, and I needed air. He held on to me and took me down. I knew enough to equalize the pressure, or my eardrums would've burst. The next thing I knew, I woke up in this place where I could breathe. I'm not supposed to tell you about it."

She took a deep breath and exhaled as she stared out to sea, again. "'Bob' said he's never seen any human so brave. He said that's one of the signs. He says I have The Gene. Do you know about The Gene?"

"I'm not supposed to, but yes," Brickley replied, more stunned than ever.

"He says I'm the biggest turn-on he's ever had!" She shook her head dreamily, then gushed, "God, just think of it!"

"You can't have The Gene. You're too nice!" Brickley blurted.

"No, I'm not. I'm a predator. I always have been. I'm one of them, Bob Brickley. I belong with them."

A steady moan began to leak from Brickley's mouth, and in the distance, the Tuckernut foghorn moaned, too.

* * * *

The next afternoon was cold and cloudy. Toward evening, the fog once again locked all creation in its grip. In the parking lot at West Beach, Bob Brickley waited for Patti Shipley. He listened to the sloshing thump of the waves breaking harmlessly against the shore, and he was relieved that they sounded very manageable, although the visibility would be nil. He had put on his stinking, seven-millimeter wet-suit quickly, and it squashed his testicles mercilessly. After a brief struggle to ease the pressure on his scrotum, Brickley decided that it was impossible to make the necessary readjustments without taking off the suit.

Oh, well. Mishap number one.

He stared hard toward the sound of the waves, gazing toward some vast, distant point as he anticipated what he hoped would be the beginning of the end of all this lunacy, and what he feared would be his death. He strapped his serrated diver's knife to his leg.

"Yeah, right!" he uttered sarcastically as he pictured himself trying to use it while "Bob" is tearing him to shreds. Then, he looked at the two big, loaded sacks lying at his feet. Each sack had a plastic flotation device. His stomach tightened, and he wanted badly to run away, preferably to the Midwest.

A red Mustang pulled up. Next to the driver was the silhouette of a passenger, sitting ramrod straight, with two pointed ears rising like triangles. Patti Shipley waved. Fritz didn't.

"Oh, shit. Not that damn dog!" Brickley muttered.

Shipley climbed out and opened the passenger door. The megalomaniac German shepherd swaggered from his personal staff car and sniffed at the sandy parking lot, making it a point to ignore Brickley completely.

"You ready?" asked Shipley, who had agreed to help

Brickley meet the "enforcer's" demands.

"Yeah," Brickley answered, stepping out of Fritz's way as the dog went to smell the ground right where Brickley was standing, probably, he thought, just to demonstrate which was the dominant male.

The distant look returned to Brickley's face. "I'm scared shitless, Patti. I mean, I have to go back in there and meet this crazy monster? He blames me for his—people—dying, for God's sake!"

He stopped short of telling Shipley about his meeting with Joya Wolf. Best that everyone continue to think she was dead.

"So, you've got the collateral?" Patti asked, gesturing to the bags.

"Yeah, I do. This all just keeps getting weirder."

Each hefted one of the thirty-pound sacks and began trudging down the boardwalk toward the beach. Fritz sniffed the sacks with great interest the entire way. The surf line was barely visible as the fog swirled thicker. All three stood together in silence. Then, in the distance, the foghorn sounded.

Brickley began the struggle of fitting on his diving hood, but when he got to his ears he realized that there was no way they were healed enough to withstand the force of the squeeze.

Okay, so one more thing's gone wrong. No wet suit hood, and saltwater in the wound, again. Mishap number two.

Shipley brightened. "Wait a minute! I've got a bathing cap in my car. Hang on. I'll get it." Fritz turned to follow her. "No, no, Fritzie. You stay here. Mommy will be right back! Stay, boy."

She disappeared down the boardwalk, and then Fritz turned and finally acknowledged Brickley's presence by way of a stare-down contest as he guarded the walkway.

Brickley averted his gaze and didn't move a muscle. After an eternity, both heard the *thump, thump, thump* of Shipley's feet prancing back up the wooden walkway. In her hand was a brightly colored cap.

"Sorry it took so long." She held out the cap. It was raspberry pink with black-eyed Susans and crimson butterflies. "Sorry it's so girlie," she said with an apologetic smile.

"That's okay," said Brickley. "Maybe it'll help 'Bob' get in touch with his feminine side."

"Here, let me put it on for you." She reached over Brickley's head and gently spread the cap over his ears, causing immediate, biting pain nevertheless. Brickley tried not to grunt as she adjusted it.

"Owww..." he finally groaned.

"Hang on," ordered Shipley, working out a wrinkle. "Okay. Now, you're ready."

Brickley finally exhaled. "I guess it's time."

He would trade what he was about to do for a root canal with no anesthesia.

"I wish we didn't have to meet out at that rock." He nodded to the spot where Brickley had his first meeting with the 'enforcer'. The storm had taken away the buoy that marked the submerged boulder. All that remained was the blue-green surface of the sea. "Why can't he come ashore? I guess I'm stalling. Let's do it."

"Yeah, let's get it over with." Shipley tried to be cheerful. "You'll be okay. I have a feeling that thing will keep his word."

"Yeah," Brickley said with his gaze now as far away as ever.

That thing will eat me.

He felt Shipley turn to him. Then, he felt her arms circle his damp, moldy wet-suit and pulled him toward her.

The familiar, panzer-like rumble came from Fritz as they hugged, which didn't help the throbbing pain from Brickley's freshly aggravated wounds. Shipley's lips found his, and Brickley returned very much to the present as she stuck her hot, slippery tongue deeply into his mouth.

In his flowered and butterflied bathing cap, Brickley was a sight to see. He felt a glow spread in his loins as Fritz's rumble grew louder.

The hell with the dog.

Her tongue pushed and probed, and Brickley's glow started turning into a full-scale erection. It became caught in the crease where his bathing suit's leg was joined to its crotch hem, and pushed desperately against it. A few strands of hair wrapped around it as well, and as the reproductive mechanism strove to achieve maximum extension, it pulled the hair mercilessly, making the image of piano wire cutting effortlessly through a cylinder of potting clay appear in Brickley's mind. The bathing suit's crease, as well as the overwhelming pressure of the thick wet-suit, pinned his member cruelly in place, causing the most painful erection Brickley had ever experienced.

"Well," he gasped, his eyes suddenly very clear. "As Sherlock Holmes said, 'The game is afoot!'"

Dragging a sack in each hand, mask and snorkel in place, and with Shipley's blazing pink bathing cap firmly covering his head, Brickley waddled into the ocean, slightly stooped, his buttocks sticking out in an effort to ease the pressure on his groin. Fritz watched him contemptuously.

"I've been in love with you since the sixth grade, Bob Brickley!" Shipley suddenly called after him.

Brickley stopped, paused, then slowly doubled over completely, resting his arms on his thighs. "Owww!" Shipley heard him moan. "Christ, please let me live through this!"

Then, he continued waddling toward the now-cold water, this time with a sudden sense of urgency. The foghorn sang. It sounded like "doom, doom."

Fritz watched Brickley's first failed attempt to get beyond the small but still formidable breakers. The first two-foot wave snatched one of the sacks and took it on a return trip to the beach. Something told Brickley not to wrap the drawstrings of each sack around his wrists. Nevertheless, the wave's momentum pushed him backward, also. Then, the retreating wash swept the bags, and Brickley, seaward, right into another breaker.

Shipley laughed. It was more to encourage him than anything else. Inwardly, she was petrified.

Brickley finally made it into the water beyond the surf zone with his cargo.

Standing in the wash, soaking wet and shivering, Shipley shouted encouragement. Within fifteen minutes, she would be screaming in horror.

Brickley floated face-down for a few minutes to catch his breath. The cold seawater, combined with the unexpected struggle, blessedly reversed the pressure in his wet-suit, but shocked his head in spite of Shipley's decorative bathing cap. Brickley had no doubt that he would soon have an intense headache.

Catching his breath, he kicked his way toward the rock. Staring into the depths, his gaze could penetrate no farther than six inches before the olive-brown murk engulfed all. The sacks were barely buoyant and still a drag.

"This sucks," Brickley said aloud into his snorkel.

His flippered feet kicked on, his breathing still laboring in spite of the rest. He wished he had a way to tie the sacks to his belt rather than carry them in each hand. Often, he had to lift his head above the water to get his bearings. Each time he did so, a trickle of water leaked in through his collar. Each time that happened, he said with sincere feeling, "Shit, that's cold!"

Self-pity reigned supreme.

Then, there was a circular rippling at the surface, indicating that he was on course. The rock lay dead ahead.

Brickley knew he'd arrived at the spot when, out of the subsurface gloom, the dark shadow of the huge, submerged, seaweed-shrouded boulder took shape an instant before he collided with it. The slow-speed impact caused a torrent of water to surge into his mask, and another cloud of butterflies burst in his already nervous, still sore stomach.

"This really sucks!" he said. He cleared his mask, blowing through his nose as he lifted its bottom.

It was then that Brickley sensed movement. Something huge. His heart stopped, and he would easily have shat in his wet-suit had his buttocks not been so tight because of it. Suddenly, the two sacks, containing sixty pounds of raw chicken, were ripped from his hands. Had the drawstrings been wrapped around his hands, they would have gone with them.

Brickley spun toward shore and kicked with abandon.

Done! Did it! Now, get out of this damned ocean and never get back in!

He half-expected to feel his feet being bitten off.

Fifty yards!

Brickley realized that panic was starting to shriek inside him.

Forty yards, and I've still got my feet. Stay calm, damnit! Gonna make it!

Oh, God! Thirty yards.

Shit, this sucks!

You're gonna make it...hang in there!

Twenty-five. Ten yards.

His feet touched bottom.

Then, it happened. An iron hand seized his right foot. Brickley screamed into his snorkel.

The attacker yanked him backward as though he weighed nothing. Brickley's scream turned into a war cry of desperate determination as he violently kicked his leg. The expensive, top-of-the-line, split-fin flipper was torn from his foot. Suddenly freed, Brickley stroked like a wild man, spray flying from his propeller-like arms and legs.

Bob Brickley didn't have a chance. He knew it was coming. He tensed his body for the biggest hit he would ever take in his life. The impact came from below and behind. It thrust him clear out of the water, his rag-doll body barely visible in an explosion of spray, while his brilliantly decorated bathing cap glowed like a floral beacon. On the beach less than a hundred feet away, Shipley screamed and screamed.

Brickley's hands instinctively grasped his abdomen when it was torn open, pouring its contents into the sea. Blood, gore—his entrails hanging out like jellyfish tentacles. Oddly, he didn't feel a thing beyond the usual throbbing ear, stomach, head, and crotch.

What the...

Brickley's hands discovered that his guts were not only still inside his body, but that a blunt object had been thrust against his sore stomach. It was his long-lost spear gun! Could it be that the monster actually intended to fulfill his part of the bargain?

The "enforcer's" half-shark, half-human face slowly rose out of the water, enough for its massive nose to almost touch Brickley's.

"My end of the deal, you fuckin' dick!" the creature hissed with its ghastly breath, then swung around and aimed a commanding finger at the hysterically shrieking Patti Shipley, who was splashing into the water in an instinctive attempt to rescue Brickley yet again.

"Shut up!" it roared.

Shipley froze where she was and clapped both hands over her mouth.

A courage he was starting to get used to rose up in Brickley's pounding heart.

"Don't talk to her that way, you son of a bitch!"

He punched "Bob" as hard as he could, right in the nose, instantly fracturing two fingers.

"Ahh! God!" He winced.

To Brickley's astonishment, 'Bob' broke into peals of bizarre, rumbling laughter. "I'd thought about killing you anyway, but that bathing cap makes my night! Still, you stupid shithead..."

"Bob" grabbed Brickley by the shoulders and shook him like a rag doll. "I...am...sick...of...yoo-ou-uuu!"

It flung Brickley toward the beach as though he was a bag

of garbage, and with a single swish of its huge, crescent tail, slapped Brickley's $140.00 mask and $45.00 snorkel clear off his face and into the depths. Joya Wolf's new mate was gone, leaving Bob Brickley awash in fresh agony.

"Thanks for the spear gun, at least," he called absently.

As the great Patti Shipley pistoned her way through the shallow water to affect the rescue, Brickley shut his eyes, the exhaustion of the past week taking over completely. He relaxed his muscles as best he could, cradling his spear gun in his uninjured hand, and moved toward the approaching Shipley, the beach, and home.

It was then that he realized the spear was missing from the gun. Or was it? The line that he hoped still secured the spear to the gun extended into the murk. He tugged. It tugged back. The spear was secure, and impaled on it was an enormous, half-dead striped bass that lolled to the surface.

When Patti Shipley's iron hands gripped his shoulders and hauled him toward the beach, Bob Brickley had a feeling...no, a certainty, that he would never, ever see the Karkarians, again.

Or would he?

About the Author:

Chuck Daukas holds a degree in Creative Writing from the University of Colorado at Boulder. He is a native of the South Shore of Rhode Island where he was an avid scuba diver, having dived the German U-boat U-853 several times, and an enthusiastic sport fisherman and spear fisherman.

A devoted animal lover, he presently lives in North Carolina with his three rescue cats, ex-stray dog and a bunch of chickens. He is an active blogger.

Visit his website at:
http://www.alittlenightfishing.com

Also from Damnation Books:

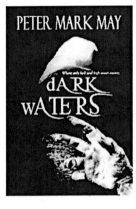

Dark Waters
by Peter Mark May

eBook ISBN: 9781615723898
Print ISBN: 9781615723904

Thriller Supernatural/Occult
Novella of 34,457 words

Where only hell and high water awaits...

The caves have been explored before.

Now man has entered the legendary tunnels again; to delve deeper than before.

But the storm waters are rising. Their way out is blocked. The only route they have left is to dive deeper into the dark waters of the tunnels s in hope of escape Will they find a way out or they answers to the mysteries of the depths Where a death scream can echo for five miles....

Dark Waters will trap you in an air pocket of asphyxiating terror.

Also from Damnation Books:

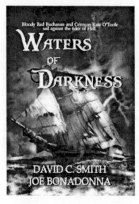

Waters of Darkness
by Dave Smith and Joe Bonadonna

eBook ISBN: 9781615729111
Print ISBN: 9781615729128

Dark Fantasy Action/Adventure
Novel of 59,999 words

Bloody Red Buchanan and Crimson Kate O'Toole sail against the tides of Hell.

1640. The Age of Pirates. Bloody Red Buchanan and Crimson Kate O'Toole sail for eastern seas and the Isle of Shadow, looking for treasure. Their galleons take them into the tides of Hell. More of their crews die than stay alive as they fight the ancient sorcery of an undying priest of Dagon and the sorcerer with efreet who follow his commands. The seas will fill with blood, and Hell will scream with the freshly dead, before these pirates fight their way free of the evils they have loosed.

Visit Damnation Books online at:

Our Blog—
http://www.damnationbooks.com/blog/

DB Reader's Yahoogroup—
http://groups.yahoo.com/group/DamnationBooks/

Twitter—
http://twitter.com/DamnationBooks

Google+—
https://plus.google.com/u/0/115524941844122973800

Facebook—
https://www.facebook.com/pages/
Damnation-Books/80339241586

Tumblr—
http://eternalpress-damnationbooks.tumblr.com

Pinterest—
http://www.pinterest.com/EPandDB

Instagram—
http://instagram.com/eternalpress_damnationbooks

Youtube—
http://www.youtube.com/channel/
UC9mxZ4W-WaKHeML_f9-9CpA

Goodreads—
http://www.goodreads.com/DamnationBooks

Shelfari—
http://www.shelfari.com/damnationbooks

Library Thing—
http://www.librarything.com/DamnationBooks

HorrorWorld Forums—
http://horrorworld.org/phpBB3/viewforum.php?f=134

CPSIA information can be obtained at www.ICGtesting.com
Printed in the USA
LVOW08s0339190714

395091LV00001B/31/P